SWEET AND SOUR

Tales from China

Sweet and Sour

Tales from China

Retold by
Carol Kendall
and
Yao-wen Li

Drawings by
SHIRLEY FELTS

 Houghton Mifflin/Clarion Books/New York

Houghton Mifflin/Clarion Books
52 Vanderbilt Avenue, New York, N.Y. 10017

Second American edition 1980

Text copyright © 1978 by Carol Kendall and Yao-wen Li
Illustrations copyright © 1978 by Shirley Felts
This book was first published in Great Britain in 1978
by the Bodley Head Ltd.

Library of Congress Cataloging in Publication Data

Kendall, Carol, 1917-Sweet and Sour: tales from China.
"A Clarion book."
Summary: A collection of tales from various periods of Chinese history.
1. Tales, Chinese. [1. Folklore—China] I. Li, Yao-wen, joint author. II. Title.
PZ8.1.K36Sw   398.2'0951   78-24349   0-395-28958-0

CONTENTS

An Extra Word,
Not Without Interest

In choosing the tales to appear in *Sweet and Sour*, we made just two simple conditions: first, that they be Chinese; and second, that we like them.

We have not tried to squeeze our stories into a theme or scheme, but have indulged in folklore and fairy tale, anecdotes, parables, fables and jokes—and one science fiction account that happened along.

Neither have we created a particular-time mould to pour our stories into. 'The Unanswerable' was written in the third century BC (the Warring States Period); 'Old Fuddlement' and several more are from the Ch'ing Dynasty, which was overthrown by the Revolution of 1911. All others lie somewhere between, not because we set these two eras as limits, but because our choices just happened to fall there.

The greatest problem in translating Chinese into English is not so much the words as the lack of them. The Chinese are not known for verbosity in their writing, and the further back in time one reads, the terser they become. Their early stories are pared to the very bone; at times even the bone seems to have been whittled away. 'Thievery', in fact, was originally told in three scant lines! Even if we accepted the fanciful theory that merely to look at Chinese characters is to read half the story, the result would still be a synopsis rather than a full-fleshed telling.

7

Fleshing-out, then, or fattening, is what we have done to these tales. We have not changed endings or tampered with the bare-bones of plot. Sometimes we have had to make a choice of several versions. 'Logic', for instance, was first told of an early Emperor and his young son to show how clever the heir to the throne was. We decided on the later, villager, version, if only to show that Emperors' sons don't hold the edge on cleverness.

We have avoided larding our retellings with foreign or unfamiliar words, but a few are too much a part of Chinese life to be disposed of, and besides, we like them. For the curious, a 'catty' is a measure of sixteen taels, which, with caution, one can call sixteen Chinese ounces, and sixteen Chinese ounces are equal to $1\frac{1}{3}$ English-speaking pounds, or just over half a kilo. A 'cangue' is a desperately uncomfortable huge square wooden collar, weighing about fifty catties, that was locked into place round criminals' necks for punishment—a sort of portable pillory. While wearing it, wrong-doers couldn't reach their hands over it to their faces and so had to be fed or have their noses scratched by others.

A string of cash is exactly that, the cash being a round Chinese coin of small value with a square hole in its middle, the string handily keeping one's fortune tied up—not so tidily as paper coin wrappers from the bank, definitely noisier to carry about, but much more satisfactory to count!

Kuan-yin is the all-merciful goddess, the bringer of children, and has been much loved by the Chinese over hundreds of years. She is a Boddhisattva: that is, a holy person who has stopped just short of attaining eternal bliss and has deliberately chosen to remain 'living' in order to help those who ask for her mercy. She lives in many places at once and assumes various forms; in fact, before Buddhism came to China from India in the third century, Kuan-yin was a male!

Three of our stories have to do with Taoism, an ancient mystical philosophy that has run side-by-side with prosaic Confucianism through the ages—a good pair for striking a balance.

'From Bad to Good to Bad to Good' appears to be a fairly simple story in itself, but it was written to demonstrate the mysteries of nature, so deep, the Taoists believe, as to be unfathomable to humankind.

'Golden Life' is based on the belief of some Taoists that the secret of eternal life lay in the swallowing of a magic potion—if only it could be concocted! As early as the second century BC, alchemists were experimenting with combinations of chemicals to make the elixir of immortality. Gold fluid was considered one of the most important ingredients, and cinnabar once it had been converted into mercury: more than one emperor died of mercury poisoning from greedily drinking his alchemist's death-cures.

The legends that were told about the elixir, however, have happier endings. By tradition the philosopher Huai-nan-tsu, who wrote 'From Bad to Good to Bad to Good', discovered the elixir of immortality, drank of it, and rose directly up to heaven in broad daylight. In his agitation at such an abrupt ascent, however, he dropped the potion cup. It fell back into his own courtyard, where the dogs and chickens and ducks and geese sampled the spilt dregs, and promptly went sailing up to heaven after their master.

9

'The Pointing Finger' is one of many Taoist tales about the Eight Immortals whose fabled home was the magical island of P'eng-lai. It was in the fourth century BC that Chinese ships first set out to look for the island. A century later the First Emperor of the Ch'in Dynasty let himself be tricked by a rascally Taoist sage into sending three thousand youths and maidens and cargoes of seeds and other gifts to fabulous P'eng-lai, which the sage claimed to have visited. The expedition never returned, but a legend grew up that it landed on an island in an archipelago and thus the three thousand became the original settlers of Japan.

Whatever happened, the stories of the search for P'eng-lai will have a familiar ring to the science fiction fancier, who has only to substitute uncharted space for uncharted seas, rocket ships for sailing vessels, extra-terrestrial life for Immortals, and yes, reports of flying saucers for Chinese mariners' tales of islands rising out of the sea only to turn upside down or to vanish, finally, into the mists.

There have been many talented and accomplished women in China's history, but we seldom hear their names. In stories of the past, too, no matter how courageous, true, and noble, a woman seldom appears in her own right. The clever wife in the story of that name has no identity beyond being Fu-hsing's wife, and while he gives full due to her cleverness, it is clear that he looks upon it, like her, as his property.

To redress the balance we have included an unusual story, 'The Serpent-Slayer', from the fourth century AD. Supernatural tales had swept into popularity, and writers were hard put to it to meet their readers' insatiable demands. They scanned histories and geographies and biographies, combed records of all kinds, kept their ears open to rumour, sought out obscure legends—all in the interest of entertaining their public with bizarre tales. Whatever truth might lurk in 'The Serpent-Slayer', and the author works hard at setting the stage in the original version (a crevice on the northwest side of a mountain called Yung-ling, which is situated in Min-chung Province, in Tung-yueh), one wonders which character the writer considered more bizarre—the serpent or the slayer!

Chinese names, when they are at home in China, are quite logically written in the order we save for telephone directories: last names come first. Yao-wen Li, however, has adopted the Western style of setting down her name. 'Yao-wen', by the way, means 'Literary Brilliance'.

We wish you happy reading.

CAROL KENDALL

YAO-WEN LI

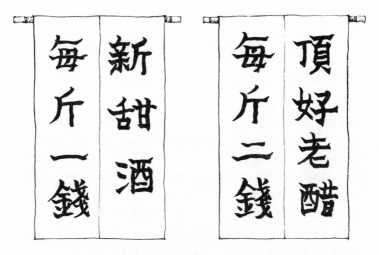

A Rare Bargain

Two friends stopped for a drink at a wine shop that advertised its wares on two scrolls fastened to the wall:

Sweet new wine per catty: 1 copper

Best aged vinegar per catty: 2 coppers

They ordered the wine, but at the first swallow they choked and gasped and spat; tears ran in rivulets down to their chins.

'Agh ...!' cried one, sticking his tongue out and fanning it. 'That's not wine! They've given us the vinegar by mistake!'

'Sssst!' said his friend, kicking his leg. 'Not so loud, stupid one—they'll charge us double!'

Ch'ing Dynasty (1644–1911)

The Clever Wife

A very long time ago there lived in a far corner of China, in Sinkiang, a good and simple man named Fu-hsing, who had an unusually clever wife. All the day long he would run to her with questions about thus-and-such, or about such-and-thus, as the case might fall out; and no matter how difficult the problem he took to her, she always thought of a solution. Thanks to her wondrous acumen, the house of Fu-hsing prospered mightily.

Fu-hsing was remarkably proud of his wife and often spoke of her as his 'Incomparable Wisdom', his 'Matchless Wit', or his 'Dearest Capability'. He only wished that all who passed his house could know it was her cleverness had brought him such great prosperity. For months he puzzled his head over a suitable way of declaring his gratitude, and at last conceived of a couplet that delicately conveyed his feeling. He inscribed the lines on twin scrolls and posted them on the gate before his house:

> 'A Matchless Wit like Fu-hsing's
> Does with ease a million things.'

All who passed the house saw the scrolls, and those who knew Fu-hsing thought what a scrupulous and honest husband he was to thus praise his wife. One day, however, the district magistrate happened to pass that way. On reading the scrolls, he drew his mouth down and his eyebrows together in a terrible frown.

14

'What a boastful, conceited fellow lives there!' he thought. 'What appalling arrogance! Such windbaggery should not go unpunished!' When he returned to his quarters, he sent a clerk with a stern summons for Fu-hsing to appear before him forthwith.

The summons so frightened Fu-hsing that he could scarce speak enough words to tell his wife of it. '. . . can't understand . . . I'm law-abiding . . . good citizen . . . pay taxes and tariffs without cheating . . .' He pulled frantically at his hair, sprinkling strings of it on the floor. 'My dear Capability, what *can* I have done to bring upon me this summons?'

His wife laid a calming hand on his before he could tear out the last of his sparse hair. 'It must be,' she said after a moment's thought, 'that the scrolls on the gate have given offence. Really, it is not worth worrying about! Go with the clerk to see the magistrate and have no fear. If you run into difficulty, we can talk it over when you return.'

Much relieved, Fu-hsing went off with the clerk and soon was standing before the magistrate, whose eyebrows by now had nudged so close together that they were quite entangled with each other. He sat glowering behind an immense table, his arms folded magisterially into his sleeves.

'So!' he exclaimed. 'This is the braggart who posts scrolls on his gate to boast of his extraordinary cleverness!' He leant forward to glare into Fu-hsing's face, the terrible eyebrows bristling like angry hedgehogs. 'You would have the world believe you can do anything at all, would you! No matter how difficult? Very well!' Loosing his arms from his sleeves, he struck an angry fist on the table. 'I have three small tasks for you to perform. At once! For a fellow of your prodigious talents, they should provide no difficulty. No difficulty whatsover.

'First, then,' and *pound* went the fist, 'you shall weave a cloth as long as a road.

'Second,' *pound, pound,* 'you shall make as much wine as there is water in the ocean.

'Third,' *pound, pound, pound,* 'you shall raise a pig as big as a mountain.'

With an awful smile, the magistrate uncurled his fist to waggle a long finger under poor Fu-hsing's nose. 'Of course, if you do not accomplish these tasks for me *one-two-three*, you will soon learn how this court deals with swollen heads!'

Wretched and anxious, Fu-hsing hastened home to his wife and stammered out the three impossible demands made by the magistrate.

His wife threw back her head and laughed. 'Foolish husband!' she said. 'The hardest problems are those with the simplest answers!'

Fu-hsing continued to wring his hands. 'But what shall I do? I know that you can accomplish anything, but this is beyond all reason . . .'

Madame Fu-hsing's smile stopped him. 'It is really quite simple. Rest well tonight. Tomorrow you must go back to the magistrate and present to him three quite ordinary implements which I shall make ready for you. I will give you certain words to take along with these devices, and you must say them to the magistrate just as I tell them to you.'

Fu-hsing attended well to his wife's instructions, and the next morning, carrying a ruler, a large measuring bowl and a balancing scale, he presented himself to the magistrate once again. When he started speaking, the eyebrows were as tightly knotted as before, but as Fu-hsing continued, and laid in turn the three measuring devices before the magistrate, the brows gradually lifted up and away from his eyes until they became flying birds of astonishment.

'This morning, as I was setting out to do the tasks you gave me,' Fu-hsing began, 'I realized that I needed further instruction from you before I could finish. Therefore, your Honour, I have taken the liberty of bringing these three measures to facilitate your task. I must respectfully ask you, first, to measure the road with this ruler that I may know the length of the cloth I must weave; second, measure the ocean's water with this bowl that I may know how much wine I must make; and third, weigh the mountain with this balance that I may know how big a pig I must raise.'

Fu-hsing made a deferential bow. 'Just as soon as you have set the standards, your Honour, I shall be pleased to finish the tasks.'

So confounded was the magistrate at the cunning solution to his three problems that he allowed Fu-hsing to go without punishment, and never ventured to bother him again. Truly, the magistrate believed Fu-hsing's Matchless Wit could do a million things.

Han Dynasty (202 BC – AD 220)

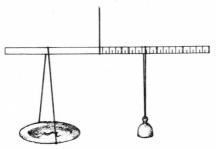

Ten Jugs of Wine

Many, many years ago in China, there lived in the same town ten old greybeards. They were good friends and liked to meet occasionally to drink each other's health and spend a long hour chatting about the affairs of the district.

Towards the end of the year, when they had all chanced to meet in the town, the one whose beard was long and silken said, 'In a few days it will be the New Year. Let us all meet at my house on the eve of that day to welcome the year with hot wine.'

The other nine old men, with a great nodding of their venerable heads, said, 'Splendid!' It was decided that each of them would bring a jug of wine, as no one of them could afford to provide for all.

When they had separated, Long Silken Beard, already regretting his impulsive invitation, said to himself,

'Sometimes my tongue jumps out of my mouth. Here am I providing the house, the wine bowl, and the fuel to warm it, *and* a jug of wine on top of all. Really, in complete fairness, I should be excused from adding my jug of wine to the bowl. The others would surely agree were they only to think of it, but I can scarcely broach the subject myself.' He ruminated further. 'Now each of the other nine men will bring a jug of wine, as is proper. If I, for my part, add a jug of water to the bowl instead of wine, nobody will ever know the difference, and justice will be served without anyone's loss of face. This is truly a way out of an embarrassing situation.'

Another of the old men, he whose beard was pointed and trim, had his own thoughts as he hobbled home. 'My brewing this year is so sour that I am quite ashamed of it. Now why should I spoil the warming bowl with a sour brew? Better for all of us if I were to add good sweet water instead of my poor wine. As the other nine will bring jugs of their good wine, really it will be quite all right, and I shall be doing a favour to all, to say nothing of the saving to me!'

The old man whose beard was soft and shaggy was also thinking of the party as he shuffled home. 'My wine is so pale this brewing, it looks like spring water. Really, nobody could tell the difference without tasting. Wouldn't it be a fine joke to take a jug of water instead, just to see if anybody noticed? I might tell of it afterwards and we could all laugh over the affair. Or perhaps it would be even more amusing not to tell at all? Yes, I think that is the most amusing way. I shall certainly take the water.'

The old man with the lank, thin beard ('I am even poorer than the rest and have such a little bit of wine

19

left'); the old man with the bristly, bushy beard ('My wine, indeed, is so weak that I might as well add water!'); and the other five old greybeards all went through the same deliberations. Even the youngest, whose beard still showed a little black, decided to contribute water in place of wine. 'For my wine is so strong,' he told himself, 'who knows what might happen to those poor old greybeards on the way home? They might stumble and fall and spend the night in an icy ditch to the detriment of their fragile old bones. I should be a proper rascal to contribute to their frailties!'

So it was that on the eve of the New Year the ten greybeards met at Long Silken Beard's house. Each solemnly poured his contribution into the big warming bowl and pretended an appreciative sniff at the aroma. Soon they were all seated and ready for conversation and warm wine. With bright expectation they ladled the hot sparkling brew into their cups, felt the warmth of it spread through their grateful old hands, and finally, when all were served, as one they drew an anticipatory breath—and tasted.

Disbelieving, they tasted again.

Then ten old greybeards sat motionless and silent except for the tilting of cups and the slight rasp of parched lips sipping and dried throats swallowing. Slowly, from the corners of their eyes they slid sheepish looks at one another. Soberly, oh most soberly, they continued to warm their greedy stomachs with the hot water. *Oral tradition*

Logic

Long ago, in a village far removed from Ch'ang An, which
was then the capital of China, an old man asked a little boy
a teasing question: 'Which is closer, Ch'ang An or the
sun?'

'The sun, of course,' said the boy without hesitation.

'Wellawell,' said the old man, smiling. 'And why do
you say the sun?'

'That's easy,' said the boy. 'We can see the sun from
here, but we can't see Ch'ang An.'

21

The old man thought the boy exceedingly clever, and the next day took him along to the market place to show him off. Throngs of people from the capital passed through this small village, for it was on a main road. The old man and the boy stood under a tree, and the old man pointed out this one and that one from afar, while the boy stared with open mouth at their strange and beautiful clothing.

'Now then,' said the old man, when he saw that a goodly crowd had gathered round them under the tree, 'tell us, young lad, which is closer: Ch'ang An or the sun?'

Promptly the boy answered, 'Ch'ang An, of course.'

The old man's mouth sagged in disappointment. 'But— but—only yesterday you told me the sun was closer.'

'Yes,' said the boy, 'but that was before we saw all these people from Ch'ang An. Have you ever seen anyone who came from the sun?'

Original version from Six Dynasties (265–581)

The Living Kuan-yin

Even though the family name of Chin means *gold*, it does not signify that everyone of that name is rich. Long ago, in the province of Chekiang, however, there was a certain wealthy Chin family of whom it was popularly said that its fortune was as great as its name. It seemed quite fitting, then, when a son was born to the family, that he should be called Po-wan, 'Million', for he was certain to be worth a million pieces of gold when he came of age.

With such a happy circumstance of names, Po-wan himself never doubted that he would have a never-ending supply of money chinking through his fingers, and he spent it accordingly—not on himself, but on any unfortunate who came to his attention. He had a deep sense of compassion for anyone in distress of body or spirit: a poor man had only to hold out his hand, and Po-wan poured gold into it; if a destitute widow and her brood of starvelings but lifted sorrowful eyes to his, he provided them with food and lodging and friendship for the rest of their days.

In such wise did he live that even a million gold pieces were not enough to support him. His resources so dwindled that finally he scarcely had enough food for himself; his clothes flapped threadbare on his wasted frame; and the cold seeped into his bone marrow for lack of a fire. Still he gave away the little money that came to him.

One day, as he scraped out half of his bowl of rice for a beggar even hungrier than he, he began to ponder on his destitute state.

'Why am I so poor?' he wondered. 'I have never spent extravagantly. I have never, from the day of my birth, done an evil deed. Why then am I, whose very name is A Million Pieces of Gold, no longer able to find even a copper to give this unfortunate creature, and have only a bowl of rice to share with him?'

He thought long about his situation and at last determined to go without delay to the South Sea. Therein, it was told, dwelt the all-merciful goddess, the Living Kuan-yin, who could tell the past and future. He would put his question to her and she would tell him the answer.

Soon he had left his home country behind and travelled for many weeks in unfamiliar lands. One day he found his way barred by a wide and furiously flowing river. As he stood first on one foot and then on the other, wondering how he could possibly get across, he heard a commanding voice calling from the top of an overhanging cliff.

'Chin Po-wan!' the voice said, 'if you are going to the South Sea, please ask the Living Kuan-yin a question for me!'

'Yes, yes, of course,' Po-wan agreed at once, for he had never in his life refused a request made of him. In any case, the Living Kuan-yin permitted each person who approached her three questions, and he had but one of his own to ask.

Craning his head towards the voice coming from above, he suddenly began to tremble, for the speaker was a gigantic snake with a body as large as a temple column. Po-wan was glad he had agreed so readily to the request.

24

'Ask her then,' said the snake, 'why I am not yet a dragon even though I have practised self-denial for more than one thousand years?'

'That I will do, and gl-gladly,' stammered Po-wan, hoping that the snake would continue to practise self-denial just a bit longer. 'But, your . . . your Snakery . . . or your Serpentry, perhaps I should say . . . that is . . . you see, don't you . . . first I must cross this raging river, and I know not how.'

'That is no problem at all,' said the snake. 'I shall carry you across, of course.'

'Of course,' Po-wan echoed weakly. Overcoming his fear and his reluctance to touch the slippery-slithery scales, Chin Po-wan climbed on to the snake's back and rode across quite safely. Politely, and just a bit hurriedly, he thanked the self-denying serpent and bade him good-bye. Then he continued on his way to the South Sea.

By noon he was very hungry. Fortunately a nearby inn offered meals at a price he could afford. While waiting for his bowl of rice, he chatted with the innkeeper and told him of the Snake of the Cliff, which the innkeeper knew well and respected, for the serpent always denied bandits the crossing of the river. Inadvertently, during the exchange of stories, Po-wan revealed the purpose of his journey.

'Why then,' cried the innkeeper, 'let me prevail upon your generosity to ask a word for me.' He laid an appealing hand on Po-wan's ragged sleeve. 'I have a beautiful daughter,' he said, 'wonderfully amiable and pleasing of disposition. But although she is in her twentieth year, she has never in all her life uttered a single word. I should be very much obliged if you would ask the

25

Living Kuan-yin why she is unable to speak.'

Po-wan, much moved by the innkeeper's plea for his mute daughter, of course promised to do so. For after all, the Living Kuan-yin allowed each person three questions, and he had but one of his own to ask.

Nightfall found him far from any inn, but there were houses in the neighbourhood, and he asked for lodging at the largest. The owner, a man obviously of great wealth, was pleased to offer him a bed in a fine chamber, but first begged him to partake of a hot meal and good drink. Po-wan ate well, slept soundly, and, much refreshed, was about to depart the following morning, when his good host, having learned that Po-wan was journeying to the South Sea, asked if he would be kind enough to put a question for him to the Living Kuan-yin.

'For twenty years,' he said, 'from the time this house was built, my garden has been cultivated with the utmost care, yet in all those years, not one tree, not one small plant, has bloomed or borne fruit, and because of this, no bird comes to sing nor bee to gather nectar. I don't like to put you to a bother, Chin Po-wan, but as you are going to the South Sea anyway, perhaps you would not mind seeking out the Living Kuan-yin and asking her why the plants in my garden don't bloom?'

'I shall be delighted to put the question to her,' said Po-wan. For after all, the Living Kuan-yin allowed each person three questions, and he had but . . .

Travelling onward, Po-wan examined the quandary in which he found himself. The Living Kuan-yin allowed but three questions, and he had somehow, without quite knowing how, accumulated four questions. One of them would have to go unasked, but which? If he left out his

own question, his whole journey would have been in vain. If, on the other hand, he left out the question of the snake, or the innkeeper, or the kind host, he would break his promise and betray their faith in him.

'A promise should never be made if it cannot be kept,' he told himself. 'I made the promises and therefore I must keep them. Besides, the journey will not be in vain, for at least some of these problems will be solved by the Living Kuan-yin. Furthermore, assisting others must certainly be counted as a good deed, and the more good deeds abroad in the land, the better for everyone, including me.'

At last he came into the presence of the Living Kuan-yin.

First, he asked the serpent's question: 'Why is the Snake of the Cliff not yet a dragon, although he has practised self-denial for more than one thousand years?'

And the Kuan-yin answered: 'On his head are seven bright pearls. If he removes six of them, he can become a dragon.'

Next, Po-wan asked the innkeeper's question: 'Why is the innkeeper's daughter unable to speak, although she is in the twentieth year of her life?'

And the Living Kuan-yin answered: 'It is her fate to remain mute until she sees the man destined to be her husband.'

Last, Po-wan asked the kind host's question: 'Why are there never blossoms in the rich man's garden, although it has been carefully cultivated for twenty years?'

And the Living Kuan-yin answered: 'Buried in the garden are seven big jars filled with silver and gold. The flowers will bloom if the owner will rid himself of half the treasure.'

Then Chin Po-wan thanked the Living Kuan-yin and bade her good-bye.

On his return journey, he stopped first at the rich man's house to give him the Living Kuan-yin's answer. In gratitude the rich man gave him half the buried treasure.

Next Po-wan went to the inn. As he approached, the

innkeeper's daughter saw him from the window and called out, 'Chin Po-wan! Back already! What did the Living Kuan-yin say?'

Upon hearing his daughter speak at long last, the joyful innkeeper gave her in marriage to Chin Po-wan.

Lastly, Po-wan went to the cliffs by the furiously flowing river to tell the snake what the Living Kuan-yin had said. The grateful snake immediately gave him six of the bright pearls and promptly turned into a magnificent dragon, the remaining pearl in his forehead lighting the headland like a great beacon.

And so it was that Chin Po-wan, that generous and good man, was once more worth a million pieces of gold.

Oral tradition

The Thief Who
Kept His Hands Clean

Long years ago in south China there lived a magistrate called Chen whose wisdom equalled his love of justice. He was admired and revered by all the honest people under his rule.

One night there was a great robbery in the district. The constable, eager to win the admiration of Magistrate Chen, quickly swept up every possible suspect in the neighbourhood and crammed the lot of them into the courtroom. He then set himself to questioning each in turn, asking the whereabouts and the wherefores and the whens and whats, until he had amassed so many twists of fact that he was quite entangled in them. At last he had to admit defeat and, as on many another occasion, he turned the hopeless jumble over to the magistrate.

At the preliminary hearing, Magistrate Chen heard the charges, but instead of questioning the suspects, he announced, 'Upon the eastern hill in the Temple of the Great Buddha there is an old bronze bell which will tell us who the robber is.'

Thereupon he sent the constable's men to transport the bell from the temple to the court, and gave orders for a blue cotton canopy to be spread on poles above it. The night before the trial he himself set firepots in the four quarters round the bell and lit them. When the fires finally died away, he slowly lowered the blue canopy until the bell was completely hidden in its folds.

Because Magistrate Chen's judgments were famous, people thronged to the courtroom the next day to attend the trial. There was scarcely room for them and all the suspects too.

Without preamble the magistrate addressed the suspects. 'This old bronze bell from the Temple of the Great Buddha has powers of divination beyond those of man or magistrate,' he said. 'Ten thousand innocent people may rub it and no sound will be heard, but let one thief touch his hand to its side, and a clear peal will sound out his guilt for all the world to hear.' He paused and looked intently at the suspects. 'In a few moments I shall ask each of you to put his hand under the blue cover and rub the bell.'

Solemnly, the magistrate bowed his head and made a prayer in front of the bell. Then, one by one, he led the suspects forward and watched while they put their hands under the cover to rub the bell. As each suspect turned away without the bell's having sounded, the crowd gave

31

a little sigh, but when the last man had passed the test, there was a restless stirring. The bell had failed!

But the magistrate clapped his hand on the shoulder of the last suspect.

'Here is the thief we are looking for,' he declared.

A stir of outrage spread over the crowd.

The accused spluttered. 'Your Honour! When I rubbed the bell, there was no more sound than when all the others did the same thing! How can you so unjustly accuse me!'

'He's right!' somebody in the crowd shouted.

Indignant cries rang out on all sides.

'Unfair!' 'Injustice!'

The magistrate, unperturbed, gave his beard a tidy stroke. 'Remove the cover,' he said to the constable.

The constable did his bidding.

There was a gasp of amazement round the courtroom, and then the crowd fell silent as they began to understand what had passed. The gleaming bell they had seen brought to the court was now black with soot—save round the rim where many innocent hands had rubbed through the grime to the gleaming bronze.

'Truly this old bell has powers of divination,' Magistrate Chen said. 'Truly, it uttered no sound when innocent people rubbed it. And it uttered no sound when the thief put his hand under the cover, for only the thief was afraid to rub the bell for fear of its revealing peal. Therefore, only the thief brought his hand out from under the cover free of soot.'

All eyes came to focus on the shamefully clean hands of the thief, and a murmur of admiration swelled from the crowd.

Truly it was a magic bell. And Magistrate Chen was something of a magician.   *Oral tradition*

The Serpent-Slayer

More than a thousand years ago, at a time when China was divided into kingdoms, a giant worm, a serpent, dwelt in a cave on the northwest side of a mountain known as Yung-ling. Its very size—it was said to be eighty feet long and ten feet in girth—was enough to strike terror in the beholder, and the tales of its maraudings shook everybody else to the soles of his sandals.

The serpent feasted on any flesh that it could get—fish, birds, oxen, ducks, geese, pigs, and the occasional villager. The magistrate of the district was so undone by these depredations and so devoid of ideas for dealing with them that he threw up his hands and pronounced the serpent a supernatural being. Everybody knows that there is nothing to do when a supernatural nastiness takes hold of a district, except, of course, to call in the sorceress; and, as everybody equally knows, a sorceress is always eager to take a hand in affairs.

This one sucked her teeth in deep and noisy thought and then instructed the magistrate to pacify the serpent by driving animals—oxen and sheep—up the mountain to the serpent's lair. Relieved to have such an easy answer to his problem, the magistrate ordered this done.

The idea did not work out very well, however, for the animals ran off before they reached the serpent, and nobody was willing to undertake their delivery to the very mouth of the cave, to say nothing of the mouth of the serpent, which was more to the point.

The sorceress sucked her teeth again and produced another idea. 'I have had a dream,' she said, shutting her eyes to slits and swaying slightly forward and back for effect. 'In my dream the Awful Worm appeared. So real it was that when I woke up the stench of its breath was still in the room.'

The magistrate's nose twitched.

'The Worm said that only a human sacrifice would be acceptable to it. Each year, on the first day of the eighth month, it must have delivered to it a maiden of fourteen years, alive and whole, else it will lay waste the whole district, and not one person will be spared its bite!'

As the magistrate was about to speak, she hastened on: 'Such a wise and clever magistrate can see at once that one maiden is a small price to pay to spare an entire district of people. Their fear is now so great that they talk of petitioning the King himself for relief.'

The magistrate was not one to be found derelict in his duty, especially by the King, and he wisely and cleverly agreed to the yearly sacrifice of one very small maiden.

The sorceress was a fine business woman and soon grew fat on the bribes taken from rich people who wanted their fourteen-year-old daughters spared a cruel death. For only a fraction of the collected sums she was able to buy a maiden from a family so poor that losing a child today meant only not losing her through starvation tomorrow. And so the years went by, nine of them, and if the serpent still marauded the farmyards and occasionally carried off a less-than-nimble villager, the sorceress paid out a small part, a *very* small part, of her gains to the bereft family to allay their grief.

The sacrifices went on until the year that Li Chi turned fourteen. Chi was the eldest of six daughters in a poor family. As the offering day drew near, the maiden went to her parents and knelt down. 'My father and mother,' she said, 'I have thought about our sad lot, with so many hungry mouths and no son in the family, and I will go to the serpent this year. The sorceress will give you money, and there would be one less mouth to feed, one less daughter to find a dowry for.'

Her parents were dismayed and forbade her to speak further on the subject. Chi pretended to acquiesce, knowing they would never consent, but she left home secretly and gave herself into the hands of the sorceress.

The sorceress was delighted to find such a willing victim, for besides its being an exhausting thing waiting through tearful farewells of families to their daughters, there happened to be a great shortage of fourteen-year-olds that year—she suspected that even the poor people were hiding their tender offspring. She graciously agreed, therefore, to request from the town officials the items that Chi wanted: a good sword, a fearless hunting dog, fire-making flint, and a quantity of food; and directly bound the bargain by sending a sum of money round to Chi's parents.

On the first day of the eighth month, the sorceress panted (she had grown most awfully fat from rich living) halfway up the mountain with Chi, the dog, the sword, and the bundle of provisions. There she pointed out the rest of the way to the serpent's lair, and left with a jaunty wave of her hand, glad to have discharged her duty for the year, and even happier to be rid of the dog's growling. Dogs always growled at her.

The trail of a serpent eighty feet long and ten feet around is easy to follow, and Chi quickly traced her way to the cave. There could be no doubt of its being the serpent's lair, for from its inky blackness there emanated a stench so foul as to almost form the shape of the worm before her. Even the fearless dog drew back from it, and when a lengthy sough of breathing from the cave disturbed the stillness, he looked nervously at his new mistress.

Quickly, before she could lose heart, Chi found a flat stone and built round it a good hot fire of twigs and branches. While still the serpent slept its heavy midday slumber, she took from the bundle a jar of sweet flour, a pot of honey, and a lotus-wrapped packet of riceballs.

The dog watched all that she did, cocking his head this way and that way as she sprinkled the sweet flour on the heated stone; when the flour had browned, she poured the honey over it and stirred the two together with a stick. Then she dropped the riceballs into the mixture, and such a delectable aroma rose that the air fairly sang with it.

So ambrosial a scent quickly engulfed the odour of worm, and no sooner did this happen than the soughing of breath inside the cave broke off. The short silence was replaced by an ominous slithering sound.

The slithering turned into a rasping, and then, suddenly, from the cave reared a grisly head. It was as big as a grain bin, set with eyes like palace mirrors, and behind it the serpent's body swelled fatly out of the cave's mouth.

Chi and the dog stood stiff-legged with fright before the cooking stone; at the last moment they flung themselves

36

to one side as the serpent, with a terrible worm-scream, launched itself in a great curling wave—and crashed full into the boiling honey syrup.

It recoiled in surprise and pain and in that instant Chi's dog sprang at it and bit off both its eyes. The serpent screamed again and humped itself to attack, but quicker than it could strike, Chi lifted the great sword and brought it down again and again on the dreadful head. At last the serpent's enormous body twitched and the folds went limp. The worm expired with a long shuddering sigh.

One duty remained to Chi. Going into the cave, she tenderly gathered up the meagre bones of the nine maidens who had been sent to the serpent in past years and carried them outside, where she tied them into her bundle to take back to the village for proper burial. Sorrowing for the young maidens who had allowed themselves to be sacrificed because they knew nothing of rebellion against injustice, she betook herself with the faithful dog down the mountain.

Even when she showed the bones to the villagers, they could not believe her story, nor would they until she led the bravest men from the village up the mountain to see the dead serpent. Then all the people in the district rejoiced in the destruction of the worm—all, that is, save the sorceress and the magistrate. The former removed herself from the neighbourhood, either by magic or by her two legs and without so much as a sucking of her teeth; the latter lost his position and fell into disgrace.

When the King came to hear of Li Chi's heroic deed, he appointed her father to a governorship and bestowed gifts upon her mother and five sisters. To Chi herself he sent rich betrothal presents and when the court astrologers declared a suitable day for their marriage, she became his queen.

The people who were saved from the worm's insatiable appetite never forgot Li Chi. Over the years her story grew into a ballad, and visitors to the mountain known as Yung-ling never after came away without hearing the Song of Li Chi the Serpent-Slayer.

Chin Dynasty (265–420)

From Bad to Good
to Bad to Good

In ancient times there lived in the northern steppes of China a young farmer who was a fancier of horses. It was a great blow to him when, one day, his favourite mare ran away and crossed the frontier into the land of the barbarians. All his neighbours and friends came to sympathize with him in his sorrow—and indeed he was inconsolable—but they found the young man's father perversely cheerful.

'Sorrow?' he said. 'Ah yes, it is sad to lose one's horse, but then who is to know what blessing might not come from this bad fortune? We shall just have to wait and see.'

Several months later the horse came back home, bringing a handsome Mongolian stallion running alongside. Now the neighbours and friends gathered to admire the stallion and rejoice in the young farmer's great good fortune, but this time they found the father shaking his head in the other direction.

'Ah, yes,' he said darkly, 'this seems like good fortune well enough, but who is to know what bad thing might not come of it?' He continued to shake his head with gloomy foreboding. 'We must wait and see.'

With his favourite mare back in the stable and the magnificent stallion in the next stall, the young man began to enjoy a life of luxury and spent more and more time riding and less and less time farming. Then one day

while riding hard, he was thrown from the stallion's back and broke his hip-bone. Again his relatives and friends and neighbours came to sigh over this misfortune, but there was the farmer's father belying their grief once more.

'Hoh!' he cried. 'Let us not mourn just yet, for who is to know what blessing is even now on its way because of this accident? Wait and see! Wait and see!'

They didn't have to wait long. Before the month was out barbarians attacked the northern frontier and all the able-bodied men were called to arms to repel them. So fierce was the fighting that nine out of ten perished in the invaders' onslaught, and many a young man's bed was forever after empty.

Not so the young farmer's.

His unfortunate fall from the horse left him unfit for battle. When everybody else went off to be slaughtered by the barbarians, he was forced to remain at home with his father, safe.

In later years—he lived to a ripe old age—when winter chills sent an ache through his mended bone, he was only grateful for the twinges of pain. They reminded him of his great good fortune to be alive.

Han Dynasty (202 BC *– A D 220)*

The Wine Bibber

There was a gentleman of old China who was a connoisseur of wines and drank only the best vintages. Unfortunately, his servant also enjoyed good wines, and did not limit himself to sniffing the cork. Thus the wine evaporated at an alarming rate; finally the gentleman dismissed the servant and vowed to find an ignoramus to take his place.

A few days later, when a man appeared for an interview, the gentleman put him to the test by showing him a bottle of wine. The applicant instantly named the wine, and the gentleman as instantly sent him on his way. Anyone who was so knowledgeable must be one who had opened many a bottle for himself! Another applicant appeared, but this one not only knew the name of the wine but described its taste in glowing terms. He too was sent on his way.

The third applicant, however, was entirely satisfactory. He was thin and ragged and bone ignorant of the niceties of wine-drinking. When shown a bottle of amber wine, he asked if it was a medicine for rheumatism; the bottle of red wine he guessed must be ink for writing birthday couplets. The gentleman was delighted and hired him on the spot.

One day, getting ready to go out, the gentleman gave instructions to his new servant about watching over the house in his absence.

'There is a ham hanging on the wall and chickens in the
yard,' he pointed out. 'You must guard them carefully
against thieves, for many dishonest people lurk in the
shadows of houses such as mine. And now pay heed:
there are two bottles of arsenic in the house; one is white,
the other red. On pain of death do not touch them, for
truly they will rupture your stomach and bring you to a
painful death, indeed.'

Lest the servant not be attending his words, the
gentleman repeated his instructions and warnings, and
then told him once more for good measure.

The servant bobbed up and down like a woodpecker
attacking a succulent tree, but his master had no more
than gone out of the gate than he killed the chickens and
hauled down the ham. While he waited for his dinner to
cook, he sampled first the white and then the red wine.
Unable to decide between them, he finished off both
bottles with his fine dinner.

When the gentleman came home, he saw at once that
the ham and the chickens were gone, and he found his
servant lying on the floor in a fume of alcohol. Enraged,

he kicked the wretched man out of his stupor and demanded an explanation.

The servant began to cry. 'Master, it wasn't my fault. Just after you left, a great cat leapt into the courtyard and snatched away the ham quicker than a whisker, and at the very same moment a dog came chasing that cat and let all the chickens out of the yard. Master, I wanted to die rather than face you in my shame! It was then I remembered, mercifully, the bottles of arsenic. Life was not worth living, so I drank all of the white arsenic at a swallow. But it was slow to work, so I finished off the red arsenic. And now, oh alas, Master, I am still not dead, but the way I feel, I am surely more than halfway there!'

Ch'ing Dynasty (1644–1911)

Old Fuddlement

A long time ago in a district of China there dwelt a magistrate who so muddled his judgments that as often as not the criminal went free and the victim's neck went into a cangue. After one of his particularly bad decisions, in which the victim was forced to pay indemnity for kicking a bandit in the stomach during the robbery, the irate townspeople could tolerate Old Fuddlement's foolishness no longer. They ground and mixed their blackest ink, took brush, and wrote out their protests in large characters. Soon every wall in town was a-blossom with their posters.

'Down with Fuddlement!'
'Useless as a black leather lamp!'
'A firefly on a sunny day.'
'He draws white tigers on a white wall.'
'Paints black dragons on dark blue paper.'
'Plays the strings of the *hsing* with an eggplant.'
'Beats a wooden bell with a winter melon.'
'Muddleheads stir the world into mush.'
'Down with Fuddlement!'

Even the magistrate himself could not help but see that his people were deeply angered. He called his constable to him and berated him for letting matters get out of hand.

'Don't you see what is going on before your very eyes, or must I tell you every move to make! The people are complaining of muddleheads in the district—there are wall-posters everywhere—and you, you idiot, haven't brought in a single muddlehead for judgment! Don't you know that the way to keep the people happy is to listen to complaints and then make an example of whatever it is they complain of! Out you go, now, and fetch me two muddleheads that I can make an example of—no, make that three: three is a good-sounding number and will satisfy the people!'

He glared horribly at the constable, who stood rooted before him. 'Your jaw is ajar, Constable. Shut it and be off about your business. I want three muddleheads in this court by nightfall, *or*—' and he leant forward meaningfully, '—*or* we shall have to make up the number from present company!'

The constable saved his grumblings until he was well away from the court. 'What piece of stupidity is this that the magistrate has thought up! Where am I supposed to find these people? Before nightfall! Three of them!'

But an order was an order, so he gathered up two of his underlings and they set out to find three muddleheads before the sun should go down.

Outside the city gates they met a man on horseback who was balancing an enormous bundle of quilted bedding on top of his head. The weight of it threatened to drive his head down between his shoulders.

'Hoh, there,' said the constable, seeing his plight, 'why don't you put the bedding on your horse instead of flattening your head with it? There is plenty of room behind you there.'

'Aagh,' said the rider in a smothered voice, 'but one must never overload a good horse for fear of spavins, you

see. I carry the load on my own head to spare my horse's hocks.'

The constable rolled his eyes to the sky. 'Take him in charge,' he told his men. 'He is surely stupid enough for the magistrate's judgment.'

On their way back to the city, they had to wait while a man carrying an extremely long bamboo post tried to go through the city gate. When he held the post broadside, the gate was too narrow for it to pass through. When he held it upright, the gate was too low. Again and again he turned the post from horizontal to upright and back again, but it stubbornly refused to go through the gate.

'Here is our second muddlehead,' said the constable with a sigh. 'Is it any wonder the people have been complaining?'

They were still one muddlehead short, but the sun was going down and the streets emptying, so there was nothing to do but go back to the magistrate with their two arrests, and hope he had forgotten his threat to fill out the number with present company.

In the big hall, the constable presented the horse-rider and the post-carrier to the magistrate and described the cases.

The magistrate nodded his head sagely. 'This is well done, Constable.' He pointed to the horse-rider. 'So you are the one who carried your bedding on your head to save your horse's energy, while all the time the horse was carrying you *and* the bedding. I am simply astounded. If you must carry such heavy loads, you should walk and spare your poor beast. This is precisely the very sort of muddleheadedness our people have been complaining of.'

He turned to the second man. 'And you couldn't carry your bamboo post into town, for when you carried it upright you found the city gate too low, and when you carried it broadside, you found the gate too narrow. You are even more stupid than your friend here! What a muddlehead! Why didn't you saw the post in two? You could have been home and in bed by now!'

The constable's jaw sagged for the second time that day—recovering himself, he quickly knelt before the magistrate. 'With regard to the third muddlehead, your Honour.'

'Yes, yes, the third!' Impatient, the magistrate glanced about the court. 'Where is this third simpleton?'

The constable hesitated, swallowed, and then, with the respect due to his superior's position, touched his head to the floor.

'Just as soon as the next magistrate has taken over,' he promised fervently, 'your humble servant will arrest the third.'   *Ch'ing Dynasty (1644–1911)*

Bagged Wolf

One hard winter's day a lean, lank wolf was prowling the mountains in search of food. He was weak with hunger and had already missed two kills when suddenly he saw, munching unconcernedly on a patch of grass, the biggest, fattest, tastiest-looking rabbit he had seen all winter. His stomach fairly ached with longing, but he advanced carefully. In one more moment he would be sinking his teeth into the rabbit's soft neck . . . He went rigid at the rumbling sound of galloping horses. Looking over his shoulder, he saw Lord Chao himself bearing down upon him at the head of a hunting party. Lord Chao! Everyone knew of Lord Chao's prowess with bow and arrow. Where Lord Chao aimed, there Lord Chao struck!

Like an arrow himself, the wolf sprang into the air. He was too late; Lord Chao's arrow was already on its way. It caught him in his hind leg. With a yelp of pain the wolf faltered, but there was no time to nurse the wound. He gave himself a strong push with his good hind leg and shot off down the mountain path. Lord Chao raised a fierce cry, and the whole party came thundering after him.

At this very time there was on the mountain path a certain Tung Kuo on his way to the capital. With his book bag, which was his sole belonging, he rode on a tired skinny donkey, and love was in his mind—love for every

human being under the sun. He belonged to a brother-
hood that believed peace and happiness would come to
the world if everyone would practise self-denial for the
good of his fellow men. Tung Kuo, being a devoted
disciple in this belief, positively ached to practise
benevolence. When he saw clouds of dust rising from the
ground far away, and heard noises like roaring drums, his
first thought was that he might even now be put to the
test of loving-kindness.

The wolf, an arrow dragging from his hind leg and
blood tracing the dust behind him, came plump in front of
him.

'O Merciful Sir!' the beast gasped, 'please take pity on
me. Save me from Lord Chao!' His chest heaved with the
effort to get the words out. 'Save me, and I shall repay you
in my heart as long as I live!'

The sad sight of the suffering wolf would have
unlocked a much stonier heart than Tung Kuo's. 'Fear
nothing, my good friend,' he said. 'Even though I myself
should be killed by Lord Chao, I shall not deliver you into
his bloody hands. I am a follower of the great philosopher
Mo-tzu and obey his teachings of love for all mankind, er,
and wolfkind.' He had climbed off his donkey and knelt
beside the wolf. 'Be patient and bear a little pain, my good
fellow. I must first remove the arrow.' Gently, he pulled
the arrow from the beast's hind leg.

'Hurry! Hurry!' the wolf cried impatiently. 'They are
coming closer and closer. I must hide!' He looked about
him with eyes of desperation, and then stared at the bag
on the donkey's back. 'There! Empty out that bag and I'll
hide in it.'

Obligingly Tung Kuo emptied all the books from his

bag and, taking hold of the wolf's scruff, started stuffing him head first into the bag. Very shortly he had a bag full of wolf, except for the hind legs. They sprawled stubbornly out of the top. Hauling the wolf out, he stuffed the spindly hind legs in first, but then he ended with a pointed mouth and black nose jutting out. Head first, hind legs hanging out; legs first, nose showing—he tried and tried again, but he couldn't get everything belonging to the wolf inside the bag.

The distant cloud of dust was growing bigger and closer. Desperately, the wolf cried, 'Tie my legs together, stupid! Anything! But hurry! Hurry!'

With the rope from round his waist, Tung Kuo tied up the wolf's legs, and tugging and shoving, managed finally to stuff all of him into the bag. Then he picked up the scattered books and crammed them in wherever he could find space—between the wolf's front and hind legs, under his nose, against his flanks, on top of his head. At last he got the bag closed and, with his remaining strength, heaved it up on the donkey's back. He was scarcely able to totter along the path from weakness, and had indeed moved only twenty footfalls when his way was blocked by Lord Chao himself, looming high on his horse.

'Have you seen a wolf?' Lord Chao demanded harshly. 'A wounded wolf?'

Tung Kuo tried to keep his voice steady. 'A wounded wolf, my Lord? A wolf is a very cunning animal. He would not run on an open way like this. Have you looked into the hidden paths in the woods?'

Lord Chao scowled down at him. 'I know your kind,' he said. 'All melting heart and wet cheeks.' Suddenly

51

drawing his sword from its scabbard, Lord Chao with a fearful stroke whipped it against a nearby sapling, which fell instantly to the ground. Then he pointed the tip of the sword at Tung Kuo's throat. 'Such is the fate of anything that earns my displeasure. Should you find this wolf and aid him in any way to escape me, I shall be mightily displeased with you! Do you understand?'

Quaking, Tung Kuo tried to jerk his eyes from the glittering sword. 'Oh, yes, my Lord, I understand very well. I should not like to suffer such a fate, you may depend on that!'

No sooner had the pounding of hooves died away than the wolf began a great noise. 'Let me out, let me out! Hurry, will you! I am smothering to death!'

In the urgency of freeing the poor wolf, Tung Kuo let his own fear of Lord Chao slip from his mind. The wolf, however, with his feet squarely on the ground once more, looked up into Tung Kuo's face with a wicked grin.

'Dear Benevolent Sir, thank you for saving my life from Lord Chao. Unfortunately you have not saved it all the way. Not having eaten this entire day, I am perishing of hunger. If I do not have something to eat soon, I shall die and your effort at saving me will have been in vain. As a matter of fact,' he went on cunningly, 'I would rather be killed by Lord Chao and served on the table of a nobleman than be starved to death on the roadside and devoured by foul scavengers. As you are such a true advocate of universal love, you won't mind giving up your life to save mine!'

Tung Kuo had no time to reason. With mouth wide open and tongue slavering over his polished white teeth, the wolf charged right at him. The scholar leapt behind his donkey, and from that point dodged the wolf's assaults by jumping to the left or to the right as the animal lunged at him.

When the wolf stood still for a moment with lowered head and panting breath, Tung Kuo reproached him. 'When you begged me to save you, did you not say that you would be grateful and would repay me? Now you are safe and sound, you try to eat me. What an ungrateful wolf you are!'

'Not ungrateful,' said the wolf craftily, 'but a wolf, to be sure. Human beings are the natural enemies of wolves and must be eaten at every opportunity.'

'I can scarcely agree with you there,' said Tung Kuo. He was thinking furiously. The sun was no longer high. When it went down, and the wolves came in packs, he would surely be eaten. He cleared his throat. 'As we are both rather winded from all this dashing and dodging about, permit me to propose a solution. The old custom in the case of a dispute is to seek the wisdom of three elders. Let us do that. Their judgments will decide whether you should eat me or not. If they all say "yes", I shall of course oblige.'

'Very well,' said the wolf, 'and fair enough. I am weary of all this sparring about. Let us go in search of three elders, then.'

They trod on peacefully for a while, but the wolf quickly grew restless when they met nobody on the path. He came to a stop in front of an old tree with most of its branches chopped off.

'We'll ask this tree.'

'Ask a tree! Whoever heard of—'

'I am HUNGRY,' growled the wolf. 'Go on and ask

before I forget myself.'

Tung Kuo hastily bowed to the tree and, from beginning to now, related the whole incident in all its details. 'And so,' he asked at the end of the recital, 'is it your opinion that the wolf should eat me after all?'

A booming voice issued from the tree, and Tung Kuo stepped hastily back. 'Now that you have told me what you think is a piteous tale, let me tell you about *me*. You could hardly guess that I am an apricot tree. The gardener planted me from a seed, and within a year I gave flowers; a few years later I gave fruit. In ten years my trunk was as big as the gardener's arms about me. The gardener sold my fruits, rested in my shade, and made a great profit. But now I am old and dying and can give no more fruit or thick shade. The only time the gardener comes to me is to cut off more of my limbs for firewood. I have repeatedly begged him to pity my old age and spare me the gashes of his axe and hatchet, but he turns a deaf ear. All my good services mean nothing to him! And you ask *me* whether this wolf in his desperate plight of starvation shouldn't eat you? I say yes! Eat, eat! And when he is finished, may he find the gardener and make a hearty meal of him too!'

Saliva drooling from his jaws, the wolf leapt up to attack Tung Kuo on the spot.

'Not just yet!' said Tung Kuo sternly. 'You made an agreement, and you must stick by it. We have two more opinions to seek.'

Unwillingly, the wolf swallowed back his saliva as best he could, and the two walked on again to the sound of the wolf's rumbling stomach. After a short time they saw a tired old cow leaning against a half-fallen wall.

'Go and ask that good dame,' the wolf demanded. 'She

looks full of age and wisdom.'

'But what is a cow's wisdom . . . ?'

The wolf growled threateningly. 'I am about to start biting you!'

Tung Kuo hurriedly addressed himself to the old cow, who stared stonily at him, licked her cracked nose, and when the story finished with the apricot tree's verdict, fetched up a sigh that made her skinny flanks quiver. 'The tree is certainly right. Listen to *my* story. The farmer bartered an old knife for me when I was but a calf. I soon got my strength and began to earn a living for him. I pulled his hunting cart while he tasted the joys of hunting; when he tilled the soil, I pulled the plough. I gave my strength freely. In those days, you should have seen how poor he was! In his kitchen there was never enough rice at one time to last three days, and his wine jug held only dust most of the year. If it weren't for me, his wife would still be wearing coarse drab clothes instead of silk and brocade and he would not be playing the country squire with his herds of cows and his fine horses. Every thread of silk, every grain of rice came from *my* efforts.' She gave her head a weary toss. 'Look at me, if you will. I am old and sick and can no longer work, so they send me out to the field where the sun burns me by day and the icy wind cuts into my skin by night. I heard the farmer's wife complain about wasting feed on me. "There should be no waste in the whole cow," she said. "The skin can be turned into leather, the flesh sold as meat and the bones and horns sold for bone meal or even for carving!"

'And then,' and the cow's voice sank lower, 'just last night she came out here with the son and pointed her long finger at me. "My son," she said, "you have been apprenticed to the butcher for three years now. It is time to sharpen your knife and practise your art." Bought for a knife, and now slaughtered by one! That is my fate.'

The cow drew another long breath. 'You say the wolf is thankless and ungrateful. What right have you to demand his thanks? Have you given him your whole life as I did to the farmer? The apricot tree is right. The wolf should eat you. And I can think of some other morsels for his next meal.'

With a joyous snarl, the wolf bared his pointed teeth and made to spring upon Tung Kuo, but the scholar stayed him with an upraised hand. 'Not yet!' he said with all the sternness he could bring out of his quivering heart. 'There is still more advice to seek, and I believe I see an elder approaching us even now. I shall speak to him.'

Tung Kuo ran ahead of the wolf to meet the old man coming towards them. He had silvery white hair and a long silvery beard, and he carried a staff in his hand.

'O my Venerable Sir,' Tung Kuo cried out, 'how glad I am to see a fellow man! Only a wise elder like yourself can save me.'

'That is possible,' said the old man gravely. 'What is your trouble, my good friend?'

'It is like a nightmare,' began Tung Kuo. 'This morning when I was on my way to the capital I met this wolf who begged me to save him from Lord Chao's arrows and I did. Can you believe that when the wolf came out safe and sound, he demanded a meal of my body! I finally persuaded him to seek the wisdom of three elders before taking the first bite, but O Sir, that has been another nightmare until now. The wolf insisted that we ask an old apricot tree and an old cow. Both of them bear grudges against men, so of course they sided with the wolf. And now at last heaven is beginning to show pity on me. Only your great wisdom can save me from becoming wolf-fodder.'

The wise old man shook his head and pointed his staff at the wolf. 'Tung Kuo saved your life, did he not? And you want to repay him by eating him up? Miserable creature who fears neither man nor God! Ungrateful and thankless beast! Scamp back to your den lest I kill you with this stick!'

'Oh, no, not yet, Venerable One,' the wolf pleaded. 'You have heard only half the story. Be fair and listen to my side as well. You see, Tung Kuo *pretended* to save me, but deep in his heart he planned to kill me all along by tying up my legs and crushing me into his bag with his books. To make certain, he closed the bag tight to suffocate me. Further, my stomach was doubled up and my back sprained with having to curve it. It is a surprise that I came out alive at all! Now tell me, wise old gentleman, does he not deserve to be eaten?'

The old man looked questioningly at Tung Kuo. 'If this is the case, then you are also to blame.'

Tung Kuo was alarmed by the old man's sudden change of attitude. 'But good sir, you must see that the wolf—'

'Please be quiet,' the wise man said sternly. 'I am really confused and don't know whom to believe. I have got it firmly in mind as far as the wolf's being wounded by Lord Chao and seeking help from Tung Kuo, but after that I begin to get muddled. Would you be so kind as to re-enact the scene for me so that I can see the whole thing for myself and make my fair judgment on who was saved or who was suffocated and beaten half to death by books.'

Both the wolf and Tung Kuo were eager to oblige. Tung Kuo tied up the wolf's legs and shut him up tightly in the bag while the wise old man nodded his head sagely.

When the wolf was secure, the wise old man bent towards Tung Kuo. 'Have you a dagger?' He made a stabbing motion towards the sack.

Tung Kuo stared at him aghast. 'You don't mean that I should *kill* him!'

The wise old man gave a scornful snort. 'Will you then release him to eat the both of us? No matter what my judgment is, do you think the wolf will let you reach the capital when you are the only meal in sight? Even if you leave him tied up here in your sack, how long before he eats through your precious books and the rope round his legs and is hot-tongued on your trail? Humane you are— there is no question of that—but you are also worse than a fool. You would remove one humane soul from the world and leave in its place a devil-hearted fiend that preys on humanity.'

Tung Kuo slowly drew his dagger from its sheath and looked from it to the humpy bookbag, still undecided. Were the years of teaching and learning to end in the thrust of a dagger into a living being's hide, or—and he smiled grimly—in the thrust of sharp claw and pointed fang into his own living hide? His hide and how many others after he had been gulped down? The bookbag stirred. There was a sound as of teeth gnawing on rope . . .

Tung Kuo killed the wolf.

Ming Dynasty (1368–1644)

The Pointing Finger

Even P'eng-lai has its tedious days, and when time hung heavy over that fairy mountain isle in the Eastern Sea, the Eight Immortals that dwelt there remembered and talked of their previous existence as mortals on earth. Upon occasion they took disguise and transported themselves from P'eng-lai to their old world to nose about in human affairs in hope of discovering improvements in human nature. On the whole, however, they found the mortals of today to have the same shortcomings and the same longcomings as those of yesterday.

It came about that one of the Immortals, on such a nosing-about expedition, was seeking an unselfish man. He vowed that when he found a man without the taint of greed in his heart, he would make of him an Immortal on the spot and transport him to P'eng-lai Mountain. Forthwith.

His test for avarice was simple. Upon meeting a foot-traveller in lane or road, he would turn a pebble into gold by pointing his finger at it. He would then offer the golden pebble to the traveller.

The first person he met accepted the pebble eagerly, but then, turning it over and over between his fingers, his eyes beginning to gleam and glint, he said, 'Can you do the same thing again? To those?' and he pointed at a small heap of stones at their feet.

The Immortal shook his head sadly and went on.

The second person looked at the proffered golden pebble long and thoughtfully. 'Ah,' he finally said, his eyes narrowed in calculation, 'but this is a fine thing you would give me. It will feed my family for a year, and feed them well, but what then? Back to rice water and elm bark? That would be a cruelty. How could I face their tears and laments? Kind Sir, as it is such an effortless task for you, perhaps you could turn your finger towards something a little larger, like, for example—' and he pointed at a boulder as big as himself beside the road '— that bit of stone?'

All along the way the story was the same, until the Immortal despaired of finding a human being whose cupidity did not outweigh his gratitude. After many a weary mile's walking, he came upon a man of middle years stumping along the lane, and, greeting him, said, 'I should like to make you a present.' He pointed his finger at a stone and it turned into gold before their eyes.

The man studied the gleaming chunk of stone, his head canted to one side. 'What sort of trick is that?' he asked with a frown.

'No trick,' said the Immortal. 'Pick it up. Or would you prefer a larger stone?' He pointed his finger at a small rock and it instantly blossomed gold. 'Take it, brother. It is yours. I give it to you.'

The man thought a while, then slowly shook his head. 'No-o-o. Not that it's not a very clever trick, and a pretty sight to see.'

With growing excitement the Immortal pointed at a larger rock and a larger, until their eyes were dazzled by the glint of gold all round them, but each time the man

61

shook his head, and each time the shake became more
decisive. Had he found his unselfish man at last? Should
he transform him this instant into an Immortal and carry
him back to P'eng-lai?

'But every human being desires *something*,' the
Immortal said, all but convinced that this was untrue.
'Tell me what it is you want!'

'Your finger,' said the man.

Ming Dynasty (1368–1644)

The Unanswerable

In ancient days there was an armourer in the south of China who had a remarkable gift for proclaiming his wares. It was said of him that he could sell an iron cage to the wild goose, and there were those who swore they had witnessed that very transaction. In the market people would gather just to hear him describe his latest castings; some stood for hours to be sure of a good place at his next performance.

One summer's day there were strangers to the district so that the crowd was even larger than usual when the armourer took up his stance on a platform before his shop. He made a short bow to acknowledge his waiting audience and without more ado launched into a glowing description of the spear which he held aloft: its magnificent shaft, straight as a taut rope; the snug-fitting ferrule that made shaft and blade as one; the perfect balance . . . At this juncture he put the spear atop one finger and set it spinning high above his head. The crowd gasped, then applauded.

The armourer let the spear come to rest and held up his other hand for silence. 'These things I have shown you', he said, 'are but the outer trappings of the weapon. The real secret', and he lowered his voice so that the audience had to lean forward to hear, '. . . the real secret lies in the casting of the blade. I, and only I, can cast such a blade, and when I go to my grave, the secret will be buried with me.'

A small sigh wafted over the audience.

The armourer's voice grew stronger. 'The very touch of a finger to this point draws blood. This blade is so piercing sharp that nothing can stop it. It will go through any object—be it made of wood or stone or strongest metal—no matter its strength or depth or density. It is an invincible point, unequalled, unsurpassed, unrivalled!'

Bystanders jostled closer to examine and exclaim over the sharpness of the wonderful invincible spear.

When all had finished looking and a good many had put in orders, the armourer laid away the spear and held up a bronze shield that flashed in the sunlight. The intricate carving on its face caught ten thousand dancing lights.

'And so it is,' declared the armourer, 'that the beholder's eyes are dazzled. But', and he allowed himself a small smile, 'should his vision clear and he advance, there can be no danger to the bearer of this shield.' He beat one fist against the bronze face; it gave off a solid-sounding clang. 'It is as futile to attack this shield with a weapon as it is with a fist! This shield is so tough and strong and durable that nothing in the world is capable of penetrating it. Nothing! The man who stands behind this shield of mine will live forever!'

The bystanders crowded even closer to wonder over this new marvel. All save one. He was of the strangers to the district, and he stood back from the rest. He spoke now, and his questioning voice rode over the credulous murmurs of the crowd.

'How then,' he asked, 'how then if you were to strike

64

your spear against your own shield? What then?'

The armourer started to speak, stopped; his jaw wagged once again, then fell slack. For the first time in the knowledge of the market place, he was struck dumb.

Warring States (480 BC – 222 BC)

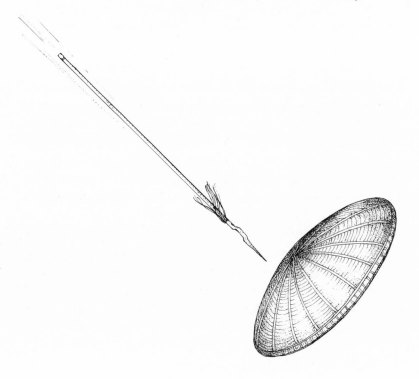

Kertong

Once upon a time there lived in Soochow a farmer so industrious that he not only kept his fields and pastures in neat array, but tended his house just as tidily. People in the village near by laughed and said he had no need of a wife—the only work he allotted to anyone else was the cleaning of his water barrel, and for that he kept a large snail 'living-in', so to speak. There were times, however, that the farmer grew morose and wished for someone to share his life, someone who would be waiting for him at day's end, happy to welcome him home.

One bright morning during the fall harvest he had no time to wash up the dishes or tidy the house before going to the fields. When he returned home that evening he was astounded to find the dishes clean, the house in good order and, in addition, a pot of steaming hot rice waiting on the stove.

'It's not possible!' he exclaimed. 'I surely locked the door when I left this morning! Who could have come in to do this?' He searched the house, but there was no one to be found. 'Now there is a fine thing,' he mused. 'If I were to believe in fairy creatures, I would think . . .'

But he didn't think very long, for he was worn out after the day's hard work, and went to bed and to sleep soon after he had supped.

The next morning he got up as usual at cock's crow. But

someone or something had been there before him. When he stepped into the kitchen, he found breakfast ready and his lunch nicely packed in a basket. Again he searched the house but found nothing and nobody. He went thoughtfully off to the fields, leaving his house in disorder but with carefully locked door.

Upon his return, he found the house in order and dinner prepared as before. From that day on, he never had to clean or tidy his house or cook his meals. Everything was done for him by his mysterious helper.

One morning he awoke before daybreak, before the cock crew, and lay thinking about the breakfast he was sure to find on the stove, when he heard little noises coming from the kitchen. Quietly he got out of bed and crept to the kitchen door. There, standing at the stove with her back to him, was the graceful figure of a young woman.

Rubbing his eyes for a better look, he moved forward — incautiously. He fell over a low stool. The maiden fled into the courtyard without a backward glance. He ran after her as fast as he could, but there was only a loud, hollow 'kertong' over near the water barrel, and not so much as a shadow of the maiden. Though he searched

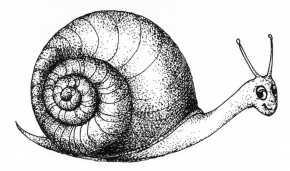

diligently over every inch of ground, he could find no slightest trace of her. He knew then that she had to be a fairy creature.

The farmer had an aged aunt who was well-versed in the ways of fairies, sprites and other such creatures, and he remembered her telling him one time that fairy creatures who took human form could retain their humanness if they were fed human food. It could do no harm to try.

Accordingly, he stayed up all that night, hiding behind the kitchen door in wait. Very early the next morning he heard a noise from the courtyard and the next instant saw the maiden enter the kitchen. As soon as her attention was entirely on the food she was preparing, he tiptoed from his hiding place and caught her in his arms. Without a word he forced a rice ball between her lips and made her swallow it.

'Creature! Dear elfin creature!' he cried.

'Let me go,' said the maiden quietly, 'else I shall never come again.'

'Then promise not to disappear?'

'Very well.'

Reassured, he let go, and she turned round to face him. He was overjoyed to see that she was very beautiful, and he stared at her for some time before he could recover himself. Then, with a start, he said with the utmost courtesy, 'Dear fairy creature, please sit down.'

'I am neither fairy nor elf,' said she tartly, 'and I don't care to be called "creature". I am here to help you, but if you treat me badly at any time, I shall leave you at once.'

'Oh, no! Please no!' He fell to his knees. 'Please do not go away. Stay and keep me company forever!'

'Only if you do exactly as I tell you. First, get up off your knees.'

He scrambled to his feet and stood before her, eager to follow her simplest command.

'Every day,' she said, 'you will go to work as usual. When you leave, lock the door as you have always done. I shall care for you and your house as long as you keep silent about my existence. Do you understand?'

'Yes, yes, anything you say!' he promised. 'Anything!'

'You must never tell anyone at all about me!'

'I won't, I won't! I promise you!' From then on, he was never lonely. The maiden taught him songs to sing, and he sang them as he worked in the fields. She entertained him with enchanting stories. His clothes— jacket, trousers, shoes, socks—all were kept fresh clean and so meticulously mended that the stitches were not to be seen. He laughed easily now, and so readily joked with his friends and neighbours that they found him a good companion instead of the old bent stick he had been heretofore. They began to invite him to go with them to the tavern, but he always withstood their coaxings in favour of going home to his maiden.

One evening, however, to help celebrate the birth of a neighbour's grandchild, he went with several friends to a tavern. The wine flowed, and too much of it flowed down the farmer's throat, where it loosened his voice. Before he knew what was happening, he was telling his friends the whole story of the mysterious maiden who kept house for him. Even as he finished, he realized his appalling mistake and begged his friends not to repeat the story. 'For I shall be in deep trouble if it gets about!'

His friends shook their heads in grave doubt. 'What

makes you think she is a *good* spirit? Suppose she is evil?
Brother, consider! Your whole life may be ruined by this
infatuation!'

'Spirits are risky,' said one of his friends in deep
earnestness. 'Even the best of them are hardly to be
trusted, not when they are inside one's house, preparing
one's food. Who is to know when they might decide to
stir in a little, well, a little bane, for instance, or something
that will make you into a spirit exactly like *them*?'

'Yes,' said another. 'Just as you forced the rice ball
down her throat, who knows when she might force
something even worse down yours!'

'Not to be trusted!' they all agreed.

Disturbed, the farmer went home. He had defended the
maiden against his friends' suspicious questionings, but
the worm of doubt had crawled inside him.

He kept a close watch on the maiden's every
movement, and took to coming home at unusual times and
getting up extremely early in order to catch her unawares.
Out of his spyings and sneakings, he was able to garner
only one small fact: whenever the maiden disappeared in
the courtyard, there was a small 'kertong', as if something
had been dropped into the water barrel.

The next time he heard the 'kertong', then, he went to
look into the barrel. There was only the big snail moving
sluggishly at the bottom.

'Oh, no!' he whispered to himself, appalled. 'Surely she
cannot be the spirit of the snail? Bewitched by a *snail*?
Oh, no!'

He set off at once to see his old aunt. He told her
everything and begged her to think of some way to save
him from the snail spirit. His aunt, a wise old woman,

counselled caution in a matter such as this, but her nephew insisted that the idea of being companioned by a snail was so repellent that he could no longer bear to look upon her, for he could think only of snail slime.

His aunt sighed. 'Then you have no need of my wisdom,' she said. 'You already know that pouring salt on a snail will kill it.'

He stared at her for a moment, and then turned and ran out of the door.

Back home, he pretended that everything was as usual. At nightfall, the maiden disappeared in the courtyard. When the farmer heard the 'kertong' he rushed to the water barrel with a cup of salt . . . but the snail was gone!

Bewildered, he slowly undressed and got into bed, daring to hope that his friends had been wrong.

Shortly after midnight he was awakened by a knock at the door. The maiden stood on his doorstep!

Completely forgetting his earlier suspicions, he received her joyfully—but the maiden recoiled from him with a shudder. 'Wretched man!' she said, and her voice struck cold into his heart. 'I have come only to take leave of you.'

'No!' he cried. 'Do not say it!'

Tears of anger and of hurt welled into her eyes and streamed down her face. 'I came to you to help you because you were a gentle, good man; I asked only that you tell no one. You broke that promise and because of your wagging tongue, you then tried to do me harm. You have repaid my kind offices with spiteful malice. You have broken the bond between us, and it cannot be patched like a torn shirt.'

The farmer struggled to beg her forgiveness, to offer his

excuses, to implore her to stay, but before a single word could leave his tongue, he realized that it was too late.

She had vanished completely.

The farmer took up his old lonely life, and again cooked meals and cleaned the house and mended his own clothes when he wasn't in the fields, but now he had a new occupation. In memory of the snail spirit, he raised many a family of snails in his water barrel, daring to hope that one day he would again hear a happy 'kertong' in his courtyard.

If he did, of course, he never told anyone.

Original version attributed to
T'ao Ch'ien, a poet of the Six Dynasties
(265–581). T'ao Ch'ien lived 365–427.

One Hairball

In the mountains of Tibet a hungry tiger prowled in search of food, but the rumbling of his empty stomach kept warning off his prey—until he came upon a frog practising high leaps on the river bank.

Too late for escape the frog caught sight of the hunter stalking him. 'If I don't think extraordinarily fast,' he told himself, 'I shall be reduced to frog sauce in a moment's crunch.'

With feigned unconcern, therefore, he hopped on to a grassy mound, sat down, and raised his nose grandiloquently towards the sky. He looked every inch a frog that feared nothing under the heavens. Even when the tiger gave a deep growl, he didn't deign to look round.

His manner gave the tiger pause. 'Er . . . I do beg your pardon, poor frog, for disturbing your serenity, but I have not eaten for two days, and I must sustain myself on your flesh before I can seek bigger game. Normally, of course, I should not bother with such a small morsel as you, nor am I overfond of frog in any case. I intend no offence.'

The frog continued to look at the heavens, but he bulged out his stomach and laughed his heartiest, deepest, croakiest laugh. 'Let me see—tiger, isn't it? Oh yes. Well, tiger, I am the king of frogs and there is not one of your kind up to the chore of eating me, for I possess skills you cannot even imagine. However, because of your great hunger—', and he cast a sidelong glance at the tiger, 'dear, dear, you *are* quite thin, aren't you, poor thing— well, then, I'll give you a chance to prove yourself greater than I, in which case I shall become your tasty morsel after all.' The frog gave a lofty nod towards the river. 'I say that I can leap the river faster than you. Is it a contest?'

The tiger smiled a shiny-toothed smile, and big droolings of saliva spilled from his jaw. 'I can scarcely lose. Prepare yourself to be eaten, frog.' He turned to face the river, tensing for a mighty leap.

As the big yellow and black tail swished over him, the frog closed his mouth on the tip at the very moment the tiger left the ground.

Landing with ease on the other bank of the river, the tiger whirled to look back across the water. 'Ho, frog!' he cried, 'and where does that jump leave *you*?'

The frog, regaining his breath from the dizzying ride on the tiger's tail and choking slightly on the tiger hair in his throat, began to laugh. 'You'll never find me looking in that direction, my slow friend.'

The tiger whirled round. There behind him on a rock sat the frog observing the heavens as grandly as before.

'Not that yours wasn't a fine jump—for a tiger,' the frog continued. 'Really, you know, I sat here and watched with great admiration as you came flying across to join me.'

The tiger scowled fiercely and put out his paw, all the claws extended.

'Never mind,' said the frog quickly. 'We'll have another contest, one that will be fairer to you. Let me see . . . Ah, yes, there is coughing-up! I propose a coughing-up contest. With the magnificent size of your stomach, you can surely win over such a small bag of groats as mine.'

On sure ground, the tiger nodded agreement. He drew in his stomach until it rubbed his backbone, and then coughed out on to the bank—only a few globules of bile, for he had not eaten in two days. Frowning, he lifted his head.

The frog cleared his throat with a tiny cough and deposited on the ground a small hairball. He looked down at it disparagingly. 'Not very much, I'm afraid. But it *was* yesterday that I last ate. I remember now. I was playing along the river when I saw a tiger coming for water. A sudden hunger struck me, so I—er . . . This bit of hair is all that is left, I'm afraid.'

The tiger stood staring at the frog. King of the frogs, indeed! King of the river bank! King of the mountain and of the plain!

Tail between his legs, the tiger made off as fast as he could, with many a backward look to be sure the frog was not following. In this wise, he almost ran over his friend the fox, who was coming down to the river to drink.

'What troubles you, brother tiger?' asked the fox. 'Truly it must be a great peril to put you into such a state.'

The tiger panted out his story of meeting the King Frog.

The fox gave a short bark of derision. 'King Frog! That's ridiculous. I shall have that pompous little croaker for breakfast! Come along, then, and I'll show you how to catch and swallow a rascal frog.'

'You don't know! You can't imagine!' The tiger nervously rubbed his twitching ear with the back of one paw. 'You will run away with fright, and I shall be left alone with the terrible monster!'

'Not I,' said the fox. 'Let's go and find this fine king.'

'Only if we tie our tails together,' the tiger insisted stubbornly. 'That will unite our strengths, besides making sure that you don't run away without me.'

Rolling his eyes upward, the fox consented, and so it was that with their tails tied firmly together, tiger and fox padded down the mountain to the river.

The frog was sitting in kingly dignity on top of his rock when they reached the river bank.

'Ho!' he shouted. 'It's high time you came with your tribute, you good-for-nothing fox! What have you brought for my dinner today? Is it that old raggedy thing tied to your tail?'

Alarm rang through the tiger's head like ten thousand gongs. How stupid he was! He had fallen directly into the traitor fox's trap! If he didn't escape forthwith, he would end up as one small hairball coughed out of the frog's throat.

With a great twisting turn he sprang into the air and, fleeing, scarcely put paw to ground until he was far up in the mountains. At last he dropped with exhaustion and lay for a long time recovering his breath. Only then did he realize that his tail was still tied to the tail of his once-friend, the fox; and that worthy was quite dead.

Oral tradition, probably from Central Asia

Thievery

With hopes of finding a string of cash—perhaps two strings—a thief broke into a house. But luck was against him, for there wasn't so much as a string, let alone a coin to thread on it! Husband and wife snored in unison under a thin blanket on a rough bed, and the only other thing in the room was an earthen jar of rice standing in the corner.

With a bitter sigh—his fortunes had been running low for some time—the thief decided that rice was better than nothing at all. He tried hoisting the jar to his shoulder, but it was far too heavy to carry any distance—and conspicuous, too—so he put it down again and, taking off his quilted jacket, spread it on the floor to tip the rice into.

The thief had just turned to open the jar when the husband woke up and, by the light of the moon through the window, saw what was happening. Quicker than thought he stretched out his arm and snatched up the thief's jacket into the bed.

Turning back with the jar, the thief couldn't believe his eyes. The floor was bare. His jacket was gone.

At the same moment the wife woke up. 'I hear strange noises,' she said nervously. 'There's a robber in the house.'

'Oh, no,' said her husband, hugging the warm quilted jacket to his grateful chest. 'I have been awake for some time. There's no robber here.'

'Hoh!' cried the thief indignantly. 'I just now put my jacket down on the floor and it was stolen! What do you mean—no robber!'   *Ch'ing Dynasty (1644–1911)*

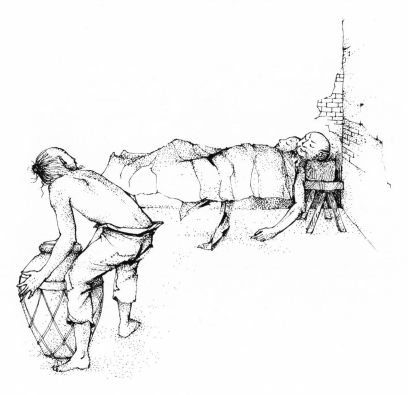

The Betrothal

Out of the mists of time comes the story of the young maiden who was left alone when her father was called away to fight for his country. Her mother was dead, and she had neither relative nor friend to console her in her loneliness. Indeed, on many a day she heard no human voice save her own from morning's light to sun's going. So it was that as she went about her daily tasks, she began to talk to the animals in the farmyard. They made but poor company: the chickens bobbled their ninny heads and went clook-clook-clook through her words; the ducks drowned her voice with their kwok! kwok! and hurriedly waddled off to the pond; the pigs squealed and koinked until she fed them, then turned their curly tails to her and noisily gobbled their food.

Only the white stallion in the stable, her father's prized horse, listened patiently to her unhappy outpourings. Tall and noble he stood as she leant her cheek against his neck. His mane was as soft as the gossamer silk of the spinning spider.

'O beautiful white stallion, my wondrous friend,' she would sob, 'I need a prince to come riding down the road or up the road, and I would ask him to bring home my father to me.' Then, dreamily, as she found comfort in the silken mane, 'And to the one who brings home my father, I promise my hand in marriage, for I long to be wrapped in

the love of one who will care for me always and forever.'

Then would the white stallion turn his head to gaze on her with soft brown eye, and for a while the maiden would feel warmed and comforted.

But the next day she would be outside the gate under the old mulberry tree looking down the road and up the road for the prince who would ride and fetch her father home. No such prince ever appeared. In truth, the only passer-by was the occasional gnarled and bent-backed pedlar too old for fighting in wars or for fetching home a father from perilous battles.

There came a day when not even the wind drew a scud of dust from the road; the chickens and the ducks and the pigs scarcely bothered to clook or kwok or koink; and the fish in the pond did not so much as rise to the coaxing crumbs she threw to them. The maiden ran weeping to the stable and threw her arms about the white stallion's neck.

'O wondrous stallion,' she sobbed into his silken mane, 'nobody will ever come to help me. There is only you. Won't *you* be my prince and bring my father home to me?'

For a moment the stallion stood rigid; then, suddenly, he reared up on his hind legs. From his mighty throat rose a great trumpeting.

The maiden drew back in fright.

The stallion trumpeted again and lunged at the stable door. The halter snapped. His massive hooves pounding, he thundered out of the stable, across the pasture on to the road and disappeared into the distance so swiftly that the dust was still whirling into the air long after his passage.

Then was the maiden more lonely than ever. She found a small jewelled snake and tried to tame it, but it flicked its tongue and glided away. She put a merry cricket in a cage, but it sulked and gloomed until she let it go. Every day she stood long hours under the old mulberry and looked down the road and up the road, despairing of ever seeing her father or the white stallion again.

Wearisome days and weeks and months crept by. And then one day, when the maiden had given up all hope, the white stallion came home, bearing the maiden's father astride his back. There was great rejoicing, and the father told over and over of the stallion's extraordinary arrival at the military camp, how he had neighed and tossed his mane and tail until the father mounted and turned towards home to be sure that all was well before returning to his soldierly duties.

Now the house was alive again with voices, and it mattered not that the hens merely clook-clook-clooked, the ducks unconcernedly kwok-kwokked their way to the pond, or the pigs koinked or snorted into their mash. Indeed, so many were the things to be told between father and daughter that the maiden no longer found time to spend with her friend the stallion. Her father, still amazed at the beast's very human understanding, saw to it that his favourite had the best of food, the finest of currying, the cleanest of stalls, and praised him endlessly for his tireless searchings.

Yet the stallion became increasingly irritable. He stopped eating. He tossed his head and would not allow his mane to be stroked or curried, or even touched. Further, whenever he saw the maiden approach, he started to jump and rear and whinny, the while his eyes rolled wildly in his head.

Beside himself with anxiety, the father questioned his daughter closely about this strange behaviour, until she burst into tears and told him what had passed. 'I asked him to be my prince and fetch you home,' she sobbed, 'just that. But many many times before, I told him that if a prince fetched my father home, I should marry him and gladly, for I longed to be wrapped in love for the rest of my life.'

Her father's eyes almost started from his head. 'Then he thinks you will marry *him*? A *horse*? Monstrous! And should I then go about the town talking of my new son, a *horse*? No, no, much as I have loved that stallion, grateful though I am for his bringing me home to see how things are here, I cannot go back to the wars leaving this affair as it stands now. I must do what must be done, the heavens forgive me.'

Sorrowfully, the father took up his bow then and shot an arrow into the loyal stallion's heart. He thought to bury the body away from all memory, but he could not bear to think of that beautiful glossy coat bored into by worms, so with aching heart he skinned the beast and pegged out the hide in the courtyard to dry.

The maiden then came to see the last of her old friend, for her father had forbidden her to approach the stallion while he still lived. She looked down upon the coat, and at sight of the gossamer mane that held so many of her tears, she burst out, 'O wondrous white stallion, I shall never marry another, for in truth I asked you to be my prince, and I shall be as loyal to you as you were to me.'

At her words, the hide suddenly billowed, sending the pegs flying into the air, and as though taken up by a great wind, it wrapped itself close round the maiden's body and, whirling and spinning, swept through the gate to the mulberry tree and vanished upward.

The father cried out in anguish and ran to the tree, stretching his arms vainly up, up, as though he could find his daughter there and bring her back, but there was no sign of her. Crazed with grief, he remained at the base of the tree day after day and night after night, looking and longing for his daughter.

Gradually his vision narrowed until each branch, each twig, each leaf of the old tree became a small world in itself. Only then, at last, did he see the small white wriggle of a creature clinging to a leaf. Its miniature head had the noble proportions of the stallion.

Spellbound, the father watched, for from the mouth of the tiny creature came spinning a long glistening white thread. This it looped round and round its small body, clothing itself in shimmering beauty.

'Daughter . . . ?' he whispered.

It seemed to him that the creature nodded. He peered closer at her.

'It *is* you, my daughter. I know it. I feel it.'

The creature went on with her patient spinning.

'Stay here always,' he begged. 'I shall watch over you, and this tree shall be forever your home.'

Again the shimmering creature seemed to nod, and he almost imagined a smile on the tiny face.

So beautiful was the maiden's spinning that word of it spread afar, and people came long distances to see her magic thread. She was greatly honoured in her own land and in the lands beyond the Eastern Seas and the Western Mountains, and although her own name was lost along the way, she became known to all as the Silkworm Maiden.

Han Dynasty (202 BC *–* AD *220)*

Clod's Comb

Long ago there lived a good-hearted country lad named Hsia-kang, but he was so ignorant of anything save the chunks of earth turned up by his plough that he was known more simply as Clod.

Ignorance, however, did not keep Clod from dreaming. More than anything else in life he wished to visit the city, for he had heard wondrous tales of city life ever since he could remember. One evening, then, he determinedly hung up his plough, strode into the house and asked his wife what present she would like him to bring to her from the city, for he was going there the next day.

'A comb!' she said, clasping her hands.

Clod scratched his ear. 'Comb?' he said cautiously. 'I— uh—what do you want this comb to look like?'

'Like? Why—' Suddenly she laughed and pointed to the new moon hanging in the sky. 'That is its shape! You can surely remember that!'

'Well, of course,' Clod said, not wanting to bring further ridicule upon himself for his ignorance. *Something shaped like the moon*, he said to himself. *I may not know much about ladies' articles, but there is nothing wrong with my memory.*

The gaiety, the luxury, the extravagant display of wares he had never known existed, the wondrous sounds and sights of the city nearly overwhelmed Clod. Truly, the city was more magnificent than his most outlandish dream of it. He wandered round, open-mouthed and forgetful of home, wife, and plough, for nearly ten days, until he chanced to look into the sky one night and see the moon like a porcelain plate riding high above the noise and the confusion of the streets. The present! He had almost forgotten his wife's present!

He rushed into a shop.

'How can I help you?' asked the shopkeeper.

Clod pointed towards the moon, riding full and triumphant in the sky. 'Like that,' he said. 'I want something for my wife that is shaped like the moon.'

The shopkeeper's face lit up. 'Of course. I know exactly what you want.' He kept nodding his head until Clod thought it might nod off. 'Round, shining, and beautiful—what better description?' and the shopkeeper brought out a round mirror. 'Would that all of my customers were so apt at stating their wants!'

Clod thought himself exceedingly fortunate to run into such a clever shopkeeper. He paid for the mirror and then, mindful of the farmwork waiting for him, he reluctantly left the city behind and went home.

His wife greeted him joyfully. 'And what is the city like?' she wanted to know.

'The city . . .' said Clod. 'Ah, the city is past telling about. It is a place to forget cares, a place of enchantment, of days and nights of joy—it is impossible to tell all!'

A trace of anxiety touched her smile. 'Did you remember to bring me a comb?'

'Of course! Do you think me a dolt?' Triumphantly he drew forth the mirror. 'Round, shining, and beautiful as the moon!'

'Round . . .?' His wife took the disc from him and looked wonderingly at it—and found herself face-to-face with a woman. She gave a shriek of anguish.

Clod's mother came running from her room. 'What happened? What is it?'

'Hsia-kang went to the city and brought back another woman with him,' his wife sobbed.

Clod's mother gave him a stern reproving glance. 'That is a terrible affair indeed! Where is this other woman? Let me have a look at her.' Her daughter-in-law's limp hand held out the moon-shape and she took it from her.

As she gazed into the mirror, her look of reproof turned to one of contempt for her son.

'Stupid fool!' she cried. 'If you must take another woman, at least find a young one instead of an old hag like this!'   *T'ang Dynasty (618–906)*

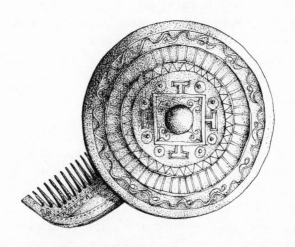

Golden Life

Long, long ago, when emperors were in fashion, there lived such a one who had everything there was to be had. To enumerate:

1 A beautiful and virtuous wife.
2 Many beautiful and good-tempered concubines.
3 Two dozen children, healthy and intelligent.
4 A country so rich and strong that neighbouring countries had to pay tribute to him.
5 Gifts so numerous that it took half of each day to carry them into the palace for presentation.
6 Fourteen storerooms stuffed with such items as:
   15 marble bins full of gold, silver and jewels of rare beauty
   50,000 catties of rice
   75,000 sharks' fins (for soup)
   90,000 birds' nests (for soup when tired of sharks' fins)
   Rare fruits (pineapple-mangoes, grape-bananas, orange-lychees)
   Rare animals (cats with elephant trunks and elephants with cat whiskers)
   Clever inventions and toys that filled three halls

He was envied by the highest councillor of the chamber down to the lowest guard of the palace, for none of them knew what it was to have every longing satisfied.

Nor did the Emperor, come to that. Having cleared his mind of wanting everything there was to be had, he found a further longing. He desired immortality—to live forever and forever. 'What a pity,' he said to his councillors, 'to waste such power and glory on one puny lifetime. I must become immortal. See to it!'

The councillors wasted no time in sending out messengers all over the world to find the secret of immortality, for the Emperor must not be denied.

After many a day of anxious unrest in the palace, for the Emperor had lost heart even in playing with the water clock and the astrolabe, there came to the palace gate a Taoist, dressed in the simple robe of his belief.

He announced that he had brought the golden grain of immortality.

It was, he said, the result of years of alchemy, the extracting and distilling of a myriad magic herbs, and there was but the one miniscule tablet in all existence. It would make of the Emperor an Immortal.

When the message was delivered to the Emperor, he ordered the Taoist to the throne room without delay.

With the precious golden grain of elixir on a bejewelled velvet cushion, the Taoist bore it in out-stretched hands and, his head respectfully lowered, advanced towards the throne room. Through gate after gate, along corridor after corridor he went, and his every footstep was watched over by the palace guards. At last he came to the inner gate with his precious burden and started to move past the guard posted there.

At that instant the guard snatched the golden grain from the cushion, popped it into his mouth and swallowed it.

90

The Emperor's veins swelled like blue snakes, and his face turned red as a fresh-boiled lobster. He wrung his hands and ground his teeth. When he could find speech, he swore that he would have the thief beheaded for his unpardonable crime.

The guard was brought in and thrown to his knees.

'What have you to say for yourself?' the Emperor thundered. 'You ungrateful pig! I condemn you to death! Speak your last words!'

The assembled guards and councillors trembled before his rage, but the guard of the inner gate remained calm. When he spoke, his voice was clear.

'Your Highness, the Taoist said that whoever ate his golden grain would live forever. I ate it; therefore I shall live forever. That being the case, it will be impossible to kill me, no matter how many times you remove my head.'

The Emperor started to speak, but the guard held up his hand. 'On the other hand, your Highness, if I should actually die of the beheading, then it would be known that the grain is not genuine.' The guard smiled gently up at the Emperor. 'That being the case, your Highness, a noble Emperor like you would never stoop to kill so lowly a person as I over a sugar pill!'

The Emperor pardoned him.

Han Dynasty (202 BC *–* AD *220)*

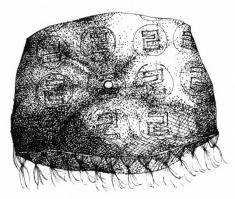

The Piebald Calf

Long years ago in Szechuan province, where strange things happen, there lived a scholar-official who had three wives but no children. One day he was transferred to a temporary position in a neighbouring province.

Before he left to take up office there, his first wife said to him, 'When you come home again, I shall greet you with gold in my arms.'

His second wife said, 'I shall greet you with silver in my arms.'

His third wife said, 'I shall greet you with your baby in my arms.'

He was so joyful at the prospect of becoming a father that he quite forgot to thank First Wife and Second Wife for their kind thoughts, and they began to look upon Third Wife with jealous hatred.

When the time came for Third Wife to give birth, then, First Wife and Second Wife covered her eyes with a cloth and beat a gong so loudly that Third Wife fainted away. Upon recovering she at once asked for her baby.

First Wife and Second Wife set their faces in lugubrious lines and made mournful sounds. 'There is no baby, dear Third. Ai-yai! We have never seen anything like it, for it was only a rather nasty lump of flesh, and we were so afraid of its effect on you that we had the night watchman bury it forthwith.'

The truth of the matter was quite otherwise. Third

Wife had given birth to such a beautiful and healthy baby boy that First Wife and Second Wife were almost consumed by their jealousy. In the throes of rage, First Wife rushed into the back court with the baby and flung it into the lotus pond. He immediately bobbed up, a smile playing on his lips. Second Wife screamed and pushed him down with her foot. But the baby was not one to be drowned. He kept bobbing to the surface and smiling, as though it was some sort of game.

First Wife and Second Wife looked about in desperation for another way to get rid of the baby. There was only the big work-cow about to take her feed.

'The cow!' said Second Wife. 'Big Cow will swallow anything. Be quick!'

Hastily they wrapped the baby in millet stalks and put him on top of the feed in the trough. True to her nature, Big Cow swallowed down everything in one gulp. First Wife and Second Wife returned, rejoicing, to the house.

In the course of time, Big Cow gave birth to a beautiful little piebald calf, and now she had company at her side as she turned the huge grindstone in the mill.

When the master of the house returned, First Wife, true to her promise, greeted him with gold in her arms and Second Wife greeted him with silver in her arms. Sorrowfully, Third Wife greeted him with empty arms.

'But where is the child you promised?' asked the scholar-official out of his disappointment.

First Wife and Second answered in unison. 'She gave birth only to a devilish lump of flesh. She should be ashamed to stretch out her arms at all!'

A devilish lump of flesh? His Third Wife devil-stricken? Without more ado, he ordered her to live away from the main house lest she contaminate others. Though she lamented and wept miserably, he would have it no way but that she should take up dwelling in the draughty rackety mill house.

When the master came to inspecting his estate, he took an immediate fancy to the pretty little piebald calf, and soon the two were inseparable. Where master went, there went calf. The master even shared his food with the little beast. The calf would rub its head against him to show his thanks, and gaze at him with big brown eyes that looked human in their love and understanding.

The master became so obsessed with the calf's human traits and his seeming understanding of human speech that one day he placed a bowl of dumplings before him, saying, 'If you indeed have a human spirit, tell me so by taking this food to your mother.'

The calf began to push the bowl towards the mill. In delighted amazement the master called First Wife and Second Wife to watch the calf push the bowl to Big Cow.

But the calf did not stop at Big Cow. He pushed and pushed the bowl until it sat directly in front of Third Wife, and he gave a little bob of his head as though to say, 'and here is my mother'.

The master's joy died at the calf's failure to understand, but First Wife and Second Wife felt jangles of alarm run all through them. Somehow the calf knew what they had done!

The next morning First Wife began to groan and fling about, and complained of such gripes and grabs that the master became greatly alarmed. Even more alarmed he was when she moaned that she would never recover until she had the heart and liver of a piebald calf to eat.

Then Second Wife drew herself up into a tight ball and with chattering teeth said that she felt the chill of death upon her, and only the skin of a piebald calf wrapped round her could warm her back to life.

The master was desperate, but he could not bring himself to kill his beloved calf, so human, so loving. All day long the two wives begged him for the calf's heart, liver and skin, their voices rising to piteous shrieks. He felt torn apart. Finally, in the secret of the night, he led the calf away and exchanged it for one belonging to his neighbour Wang. This calf was slaughtered and the heart, liver and skin given to the wretched wives, who promptly recovered and regained their old spirits. The master, however, could not forget his piebald calf and thought longingly of its faithful friendship.

The years passed, some slowly and some quickly, until the neighbouring Wang family came to the time of finding a son-in-law for their daughter. According to old custom, the daughter of the house must throw an embroidered ball from her upstairs window. He who caught the ball was destined to become her husband.

Because the Wang daughter was well-known for her beauty and charm, it was no wonder to see the Wang courtyard crowded and overflowing with hopeful young men vying for a good position in which to catch the ball.

A hush fell as the maiden lifted her hand to throw, but just as the brightly-decked ball left her hand, the piebald calf burst into the courtyard. The ball fell. In the confusion nobody could see who caught it until the calf turned and ran from the courtyard. The ball was impaled on his horn.

There was a concerted cry of dismay and the hopeful

youths fell back, daunted by this startling turn of
events. Only the maiden came running down the stairs
and set off to retrieve the embroidered ball. She ran and
ran until at last, still at a great distance, she glimpsed the
calf standing under a willow tree that grew at the edge of a
small pond. But no sooner had she set eyes on him than he

disappeared and in his place stood a handsome young man.

Abruptly the maiden stopped and then, slowly, walked on towards the apparition. At last she stood before him.

'Have you—have you seen a piebald calf?' she whispered.

The youth smiled and brought from behind his back the embroidered ball she had thrown into the courtyard. 'Is this what you are really looking for?' he asked.

He told her the incredible tale of what had happened to him, and so gentle was his manner, so manly his courage, that the maiden was deeply touched. She took the youth back to her father's house, where he told the story all over again, and at the finish asked for the daughter's hand. The father was delighted to give his blessing to the match.

Before the nuptials could begin, however, they all must go to the scholar-official's house to recount the remarkable tale once again and to unite father and son. The scholar-official was beside himself with joy to learn that he had a son and declared over and over that he would make up to him all the lost years he had spent as a piebald calf.

In the midst of the rejoicing, the assemblage went to the mill house to find Third Wife and restore her to her rightful place in her husband's house. He asked her forgiveness and she readily gave it, saying that the years ahead would be sweeter for the suffering of the past.

As for First Wife and Second Wife, they were banished to the din of the rackety mill house for the rest of their miserable lives. *Oral tradition*

Stewed, Roasted, or Live?

Two hunters had been in the field all day without flushing so much as a cuckoo; hungry and tired, they were about to turn for home when, taking one last squinting look, they saw a flock of wild geese flying over the sky. Quick as thought they unslung their bows and nocked their arrows, and stood waiting for the geese to come overhead.

'Fat, they are,' said one hunter, licking his lips. 'Think of it . . . stewed in rich soya—'

'Or roasted,' put in the other. 'I fancy roasted in plum—'

'—soya sauce with ginger —'

'—plum sauce. Crackling crispy skin—'

The first hunter glanced in annoyance at his comrade. His voice got louder. 'Rich, heavy soya—'

The second hunter returned the glance doubly. 'PLUM SAUCE!'

They glared at each other.

'Soya! Stewed!'

'Plum! Roasted!'

'Stubborn as a goat!'

'Obstinate as a pig!'

They stood glowering for a long minute and then flung, infuriated, away from each other and raised their bows to the sky once more.

The geese, with but one thought amongst them—to fly
south—were long gone.

Ming Dynasty (1368–1644)

The Noodle

A long time ago in China, there lived a very rich man whose only son was so dull of wit that no amount of money spent on his upbringing could make him appear less stupid in word or deed. His most inconsequential act ended in disaster; if he didn't spill soup down the fronts of his father's guests, then he slopped tea down their backs. To answer the simplest question he must scratch at his head to get his thoughts on the move, saying first hmmm, then dmmm, and shifting from one foot to another like a beggar waiting at the gate; even at that the words tumbled out all wrong. People laughed at the very mention of his name and called him 'that Noodle!' so often that indeed his own name fell out of use.

When the Noodle was still a very young child and seemingly quite clever enough for a rich man's son, his father had arranged a marriage for him with the daughter of an extremely proud and important family in the same district. Now, however, the future father-in-law regretted the arrangement and was determined not to give his daughter to such a dolt. The Noodle's father was distressed at the possibility of losing this excellent marriage connection; as a last resort, he gave his foolish son one hundred pieces of silver and sent him out into the world to sharpen his wits enough to win his bride. 'For,' said the father, 'the blind mendicant at my gate has more wit than my son. It must come from grubbing about in the streets and rubbing about in the countryside.'

With the coins clinking in his pocket, the Noodle left home. For two days he wandered here and there, looking in vain for someone to teach him the winning of a bride. Early on the third day he happened into a garden where there was a small pond. A gardener stood gazing into the water, shaking his head sorrowfully, and murmuring:

'Here's water sparkling to the brim—
How sad no fishes in it swim!'

The Noodle thought this sentiment was charming, so pleasingly and gracefully was it expressed. He offered to pay twenty silver pieces if the man would teach it to him. This the gardener was only too pleased to do, and proffered an additional text at no extra cost: 'A fool and his money are soon at some distance from each other,' but the Noodle was interested only in wisdom, not in bargains. When he could say the couplet by heart, he paid the gardener and went on.

Soon the Noodle arrived at the outskirts of a village. There he found an old farmer with a cart stopped at the edge of a deep stream that was bridged by a single board. While casting about for another board with which to widen the little bridge, the farmer kept pulling at his scrimpy beard and muttering:

'One puny plank will not suffice
On which to move a load of rice.'

Pleased by the sound of this rhyme, the Noodle rushed up to the farmer and offered to pay twenty silver pieces for the teaching of it to him. The old man was overjoyed to earn so much so easily, and repeated the rhyme until the Noodle could say it without stumbling. He also offered to teach him 'A fool and his money are soon strangers to each other,' but the Noodle would take only what he had paid for and went on, saying his two couplets over by turn so as not to forget them.

Later, walking in the woods, he stumbled upon two hunters, both aiming their weapons at a brightly-coloured bird as it fluttered back and forth between two huts. Together they chanted:

'From east to west the red bird flies—
Now which man wins, and which one sighs?'

The Noodle had no difficulty getting the hunters to teach him their verse for twenty coins apiece, and refusing their further offering of 'A fool's pocket leaks money,' he turned homeward, for he had spent nearly all of his pieces of silver.

As he entered the city gate, he saw a guest taking leave of his host and overheard his parting words:

'I've much to say, but time is short—
I'll tell the rest to you at court.'

His fancy once more caught, the Noodle hastily approached the departing guest and asked him to repeat the verse. The guest did so with alacrity when he saw the twenty coins and wished to add for good measure, 'A fool's money runs away faster than a burbling stream,' but the Noodle, busily memorizing the couplet, paid no attention. He paid out the last of the money to the guest and hurried on, content that he had spent his hundred pieces of silver wisely and well.

When he neared his future bride's home, he was astonished to find it brightly lit with festive lanterns and wondered how his bride's family had known he would be back this very day for the wedding. The flurry caused by

his entrance was gratifying, though of course quite befitting the arrival of a bridegroom. He graciously allowed himself to be escorted to a place at the feast.

The ushers, at first outraged by the Noodle's appearance, quickly realized the amusement they might have at his expense, for clearly he had no idea that his intended bride was about to be given in marriage to another. When they brought soup to the other guests, therefore, they gave the Noodle but a bowl of warm water and stood by to watch his face when he tasted it.

Bowl in hand, the Noodle was about to drink when he appeared to be struck with a thought, and said loudly:

'Here's water sparkling to the brim—
How sad no fishes in it swim!'

103

In great chagrin, the ushers quickly exchanged the water for soup. When the main course was served, however, they couldn't resist baiting the Noodle by furnishing him with one chopstick instead of a pair. The Noodle seemed not the least bit perturbed by this slight, but only looked about at the assembled guests and said amiably:

'One puny plank will not suffice
On which to move a load of rice.'

All of the guests were amazed at the Noodle's witty dealing with an embarrassing social situation; and the ushers, shamefaced, brought him a pair of chopsticks.

When the bride in her red wedding dress stood with the groom, ready for the marriage ceremony, the Noodle's clear and innocent voice rose over their heads:

'From east to west the red bird flies—
Now which man wins, and which one sighs?'

The witnesses began to admire this man who could coolly compose verses while watching the celebration of his intended bride's marriage with another. Clearly, the Noodle was not nearly so foolish as they had been led to believe; perhaps the girl's proud father was wrong not to honour his agreement.

For his part, the Noodle was beginning to feel bored with the proceedings and exceedingly tired from his journeyings. He wished to leave, but he still had one of his dearly-purchased verses left. Therefore, he sought out his host, the girl's father, bade him good-bye, and, stifling his yawns, recited the last couplet:

'I've much to say, but time is short—
I'll tell the rest to you at court.'

The father, being no fool himself, was quick to

recognize the threat of a lawsuit for not honouring a marriage contract. Thoroughly frightened, he turned the other suitor out of the house. With all the haste that ceremony would allow, then, he led the Noodle to his daughter's side, and the marriage was performed at once.

If afterwards, through habit, people still occasionally referred to the bridegroom as the Noodle, they did so with the respect due a man who could, solely through his wit, marry into the most important family in the district. As for the family, they never showed anything but delight in having such an amiable son-in-law in their midst.

Oral tradition

The Monk and the Drunk

There once lived a monk whose inclination, when he came up against the law, was to break it. He was known as Old Slippery, for, one way or another, he always managed to slip off the scales of justice.

One day, however, he was caught and sent under guard to the capital for trial. With one end of a rope hugging his neck and the other end in the guard's fist, it appeared that even Old Slippery wouldn't be able to slide out of the law's embrace this time. But it was still a long way to the capital; guard and captive had to stop at an inn for the night.

When they were settled down for dinner and the rope round the monk's neck loosened to enable him the better to swallow, the innkeeper brought several bottles of wine to their table, for Old Slippery had secretly ordered it during the flurry of their arrival.

'We must drink a toast to our journey together,' said the monk with great joviality. 'You are an exceptionally good guard, and I see that all is up with me now. I cannot but admire your abilities. You will certainly be praised by the Emperor himself, but, alas, it will be too late then for me to express *my* admiration, for I shall certainly be languishing in prison—and that through your commendable action. So let us drink now to your success. May you live forever, and honours be heaped upon you!'

The guard, flattered by the praise of his infamous prisoner, needed no spurring to empty his cup. He proceeded, in fact, at Old Slippery's urging and good fellowship, to empty any number of cups, until he sprawled senseless on the floor.

The wily monk wasted not a moment. He shaved off the guard's hair, took the rope from his own neck and placed it round the guard's. Then he melted away into the darkness of the night.

Some time later, when the guard came to himself, he staggered round the room looking for his prisoner. Rubbing his head to clear it, he found to his surprise that there was no hair on it. His hands dropped to his neck and he discovered the rope. Mouth agape, he fell back against the wall.

'The monk is here,' he cried out, 'but where am I?'

Ming Dynasty (1368–1644)

Coffin Cash

Poor Ah-kou the ferryman! So it was said of him each eve of the New Year. Poor Ah-kou the ferryman . . . But that was last year and the year before and all the years before that. Pity Ah-kou the ferryman for the past—but not for the future!

The past ended on a New Year's eve. New Year was the only holiday in the whole year that Ah-kou's family could afford to celebrate. On the eve of that auspicious day, the many generations gathered together in Ah-kou's shabby house to mark the event with a festive dinner. Everybody from the oldest craggiest-toothed granny down to the youngest button-eyed swaddling came to the dinner at Ah-kou's house—everybody, that is, but poor Ah-kou.

Poor in strings of cash as well as in spirit, Ah-kou depended on the brisk business of New Year's eve to pay off in full his debts for the past year. To enter the New Year still owing money was asking for misfortune, and Ah-kou had enough ill luck without begging for more!

As midnight approached, and fewer and fewer people needed to be ferried across the river, Ah-kou rubbed his tired arms and thought about going home to his family at last. He had enough money to settle his accounts, and it had been a bone-aching day. Wearily he poled his boat to the bank and was just fastening it, when a man came limping along the shore and hailed him.

'Ferryman! Can you take me to Chang's village?' His voice rasped as though every word sawed at his chest.

'Chang's village!' Ah-kou gasped. 'That's miles upstream! It's almost midnight and I must go home to my family.'

The man gave a feeble despairing cry. 'Have pity, ferryman! I too have a family, but I can't be with them this night *or* tomorrow. Come, ferryman, I'll give you a fine large sum for taking me. You can see that I am not a well man.'

That was true. Ah-kou had grave doubts that the man could pay anything at all for his passage, but he had no doubt whatsoever that the man was very ill. Ill and lame and not able to be with his family on this of all nights. He, Ah-kou, at least had a fine big family who would joyfully welcome his homecoming no matter what the hour.

'Get in,' said Ah-kou.

He helped his passenger get comfortably settled, and pushed off once more into the swirling river. Tired as he was, Ah-kou sculled smoothly and swiftly the long way upstream to Chang's village. It was quiet and dark; not even a dog's bark broke the silence.

'This is Chang's village,' Ah-kou announced.

The man didn't stir.

Thinking him asleep, Ah-kou touched his shoulder. To his horror, the man slowly toppled from his seat. He was dead!

Ah-kou stared at him in fright. 'What shall I do?' he whispered to himself. 'I shall be accused of murdering him! I must get him out of the boat at once before daylight catches me!'

Desperately he tugged at the inert body, lifting it clear

109

of the boat and then lowering it as gently as possible to the river bank. He was just disengaging his arms when the body gave a little roll and he heard the unmistakeable chink of silver. Silver . . .! Was he to be paid for his journey after all? He began to search through his late passenger's clothing, gingerly at first and then with rising excitement as he found money in every pocket—in all there must surely be two hundred pieces of silver!

'He said a large sum of money,' Ah-kou mused. 'Could he have meant so much for the fare? And I thought I was carrying him for nothing! Thank you, kind sir! Thank you! May you find your ancestors waiting to welcome you!'

Returning to his boat, Ah-kou immediately began to feel sorry for leaving the body exposed. 'For two hundred pieces of silver I should at least try to find a coffin for him so that the river rats won't bother the body.' He climbed out of the boat again.

For long minutes he searched the river bank. There were several open-air coffins, but their covers were securely fastened. He looked further, and at last found one with a loose cover that he could prize off.

He peered inside to see if there was room for a second body, but to his amazement he saw that the coffin held, not a body, but a treasure of gold and silver and jewels.

'Wonders and more wonders,' said Ah-kou. 'I have heard stories of good deeds being rewarded thus, but never did I believe them! First, I was awarded two hundred pieces of silver because I took pity on a lonely, dying man on New Year's eve. Then, because I could not bear to leave his body exposed in the open, I have been awarded this coffin full of treasure, enough to deliver everyone I know from a life of starvation. Heaven smiles upon me!' So reasoning, he transferred all the treasure to his boat and placed the body in the coffin.

With such wealth in his boat, however, Ah-kou was afraid of being robbed if he travelled home at night. He carefully hid the boat among the reeds that grew near the river bank and settled in it to await daylight.

He was just drifting off in a dream of spending the fortune he was sitting on when he heard footsteps. Peeping through the reeds, he saw three rough-looking fellows approaching the coffin.

'I don't understand where Ah San can be,' one was saying. 'He should be here by this time! What can be keeping him?'

'We can't wait very long,' said another. 'It will soon be morning, and we want to be far from here by sun-up.'

The third man spoke in an angry voice. 'We can't wait at all! Ah San knows the time of meeting as well as the rest of us. He will just have to find us to get his share.'

The others readily agreed and they opened the coffin.

'How strange!' they exclaimed. 'How very strange! The treasure has turned into Ah San!' They looked about them fearfully, as though for a trap to be sprung on them, and then seeing that the sky was brightening into day, they hurried away from the river bank.

'So my passenger was a robber called Ah San!' Ah-kou reflected as he carefully poled his boat into the mainstream of the river. 'My poor lame and ill passenger was on his way to Chang's village to divide stolen treasure with his gang of bandits. And that fine band of ruffians would have taken Ah San's share with no compunction whatever. Surely I can use the treasure to better

111

advantage. This is my good fortune indeed.'

Carried by the current, Ah-kou rejoiced all the way home. He and all his family, from craggy-tooth to button-eye, enjoyed the happiest and richest New Year of all their lives put together. *Oral tradition*

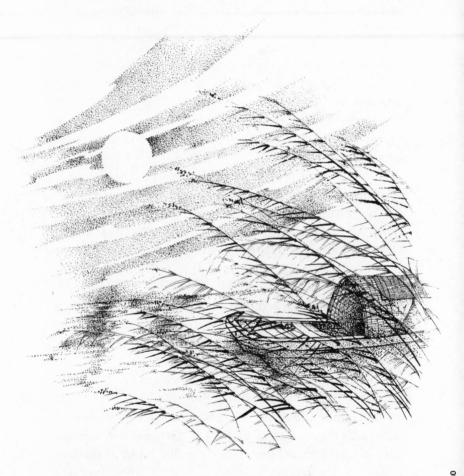